KT-365-384

CHRIS RYAN

SPECIAL FORCES CADETS

JUSTICE

HOT
KEY
BOOKS

First published in Great Britain in 2019 by
HOT KEY BOOKS
80–81 Wimpole St, London W1G 9RE
www.hotkeybooks.com

Copyright © Chris Ryan, 2019

All rights reserved.
No part of this publication may be reproduced, stored or transmitted
in any form by any means, electronic, mechanical, photocopying or
otherwise, without the prior written permission of the publisher.

The right of Chris Ryan to be identified as Author of this work
has been asserted by them in accordance with the
Copyright, Designs and Patents Act, 1988

This is a work of fiction. Names, places, events and incidents are either
the products of the author's imagination or used fictitiously. Any
resemblance to actual persons, living or dead, is purely coincidental.

A CIP catalogue record for this book is available from the British Library.

ISBN: 978-1-4714-0784-0
also available as an ebook

1

This book is typeset using Atomik ePublisher
Printed and bound in Great Britain by Clays Ltd, Elcograf S.p.A.

Hot Key Books is an imprint of Bonnier Books UK
www.bonnierbooks.co.uk

1

Bait

The jungle hissed and steamed. Great clouds of water vapour hung above the treetops, which stretched far into the horizon where they met the dirty pink dawn sky.

The Special Forces Cadets viewed the scene from the open tailgate of their Hercules C-130 aircraft.

The Herc flew low. Four hundred feet, the loadmaster had told them. The five teenagers stood in a line, the greasy stench of the aircraft fuel catching the back of their throats. Max Johnson was closest to the tailgate, frowning with concentration. Then came Lukas Channing, his black skin beaded with sweat. Abby Asher was next, the elaborate cartilage piercings that dotted each ear reflecting the red light that glowed by the tailgate. Fourth was Sami Hakim, Syrian and slight of frame, his face anxious yet steely. And finally Lili Lei: calm, serious and with the sharpest, most agile brain of them all.

They all wore heavily padded overalls and Kevlar helmets. Clipped to their chests, in pouches, were two coils of rope: one short, one long. Their rucksacks were strapped to the front of their legs. They each wore two harnesses: an abseiling harness and, over that, a parachute rig. On their backs they carried parachute deployment bags. Each bag was connected by a cord to a rail running the length of the Hercules. This was a static line assembly. When they jumped, the cord would immediately deploy the chutes and they would float down to the rainforest below.

Max felt sweat trickle into his eyes. He blinked hard and tried to calm his nerves. They had practised static line jumps in training, but this would be the first time they'd used them on an operation. And as Hector – their controller, head trainer and dour father figure combined – had repeatedly told them, parachute jumps didn't get more difficult than this. Max could almost hear him explaining why . . .

'It's the trees,' Hector said.

The cadets were in their second day of briefings. The magnitude of their next operation had stunned them into silence. They had been told that they would be in mortal danger from the start.

'Normally we try to parachute onto open ground. But in the Malayan emergency of 1951, the SAS had to insert straight into dense jungle. They developed a technique called treejumping. You land in the treetops, where your parachute rig is likely to get caught in the branches, leaving

2

you suspended in mid-air. You'll each have a let-down line to enable you to rappel to the ground. We'll give you full training in the process later today.'

'Aren't there any jungle rivers we can aim for instead?' Lili asked.

'Sure,' Angel replied. 'But the water's too fast-flowing. Hit that with your parachute attached, you'll likely drown. Better to take your chances with the trees.'

'Aren't tree branches kind of . . . spiky?' Abby asked in her pronounced Northern Irish accent.

'Yep,' said Hector.

'What if we get skewered by a branch?'

'It'll hurt. Quite a lot, actually.'

'Right,' Abby replied. 'Glad we've got that sorted.'

'Me too,' said Hector. He glowered at Abby. 'Any more questions?'

'Ah, no,' said Abby. 'I'll just leave you to think up a few more opportunities for us to mutilate ourselves in the line of duty.'

The Hercules banked sharply, then levelled off. The loadmaster held up five fingers to indicate how many minutes until the jump. The growl of the aircraft's engines seemed to be inside Lukas's head. His face was set in a scowl of concentration. He didn't want the others to know how anxious he felt. He was scared. He had been scared ever since they were first briefed on this mission. At one

3

point Woody – who, along with Hector and Angel – was in charge of the cadets' training and welfare, had taken him to one side to check he was okay.

'Course I am,' Lukas had said. 'I'm fine.'

But the Watchers – that was how Hector, Woody and Angel referred to themselves – had kept an eye on him throughout the briefing. He knew they were looking for signs that he might not be up to the job. That he might be cracking. He had done his best to remain stony-faced. Lukas was fit, skilled and an expert marksman, but he had learned that mental strength was sometimes more important than physical ability. As he stood at the static line apparatus just behind Max, ready to drop into the jungle of the Congo basin, in his mind he could hear the Watchers explaining what the next few days had in store for them . . .

'Have any of you heard of Joseph Kony?' Hector asked them.

The cadets sat in a circle on hard-backed chairs, an interactive whiteboard on the wall and the three Watchers standing by, their arms behind their backs. The cadets shook their heads.

'You're lucky,' Angel said. 'If I had to make a list of my top ten scumbags, he'd rank pretty high.'

'Who is he?' Lili asked.

'A self-styled religious leader and head of a guerrilla

unit called the LRA,' Hector said. 'He operated mainly in central Africa, and abducted more than 60,000 children to become child soldiers. He would desensitise them to the horrors of warfare by making them perform the most sickening atrocities on each other and other people. Angel's right – he was a bad guy.'

'You said "was",' Max cut in. 'Is he dead?'

'No,' Hector replied. 'But his army is severely weakened and he's thought to be in bad health. Joseph Kony isn't our problem.'

'Then why –'

'Just listen, Max.' Hector clicked a button on a handheld control and a jowly face appeared on the whiteboard. It bore scars, and one of its eyes was clouded the colour of milk.

'This is Oscar Juwani,' Hector said. 'He sees himself as Joseph Kony's successor. His people are marauding on the border between Uganda and the Democratic Republic of Congo. Juwani has a history of violent behaviour. Now he wants to build up his own army so that he can take over larger areas of land and challenge the government. His men abduct children and young people from poor villages, steal the villagers' money and supplies and force the children into lives of soldiering.'

'Bit like us then,' Abby said.

Her joke fell flat.

'Not at all like you,' Angel said severely. 'The things

these kids are forced to do . . . you wouldn't want to know about it.'

'Why do I get the feeling,' Abby muttered, 'we're going to find out pretty soon?'

Abby's lips were dry and her stomach churned. The loadie had just held up three fingers. She triple-checked the straps and harnesses of her parachute rig, then kept her attention fixed firmly on Lukas's back. The view across the misty treetops of the rainforest was doing nothing for her nerves. She'd been in some bad situations before – they all had – but this plan seemed unusually high-risk, even for them. Treejumping, the most dangerous type of parachuting? Check. And if they made it safely to the ground, they'd still be in danger. Also check. Even Abby, who was always ready with a wisecrack, had been stunned into silence when Hector had told them exactly what he and his superiors had in mind for the cadets . . .

'Two weeks ago, Oscar Juwani and his thugs kidnapped two British citizens. They were research scientists on a field trip in the Congo rainforest. Juwani demanded a ransom of ten million US dollars. What he got was a four-man SAS unit hunting him down. The unit was unsuccessful. Our intelligence reports suggest that the unit succumbed to a tropical illness which put them off

their guard. As a result, Juwani's gang captured them. Our understanding is that the British hostages have been killed, but the SAS men are alive and being slowly starved to death as a deterrent to any other foreign powers who might be tempted to intefere with Oscar Juwani. That's where you come in.'

'Some deterrent,' Sami said under his breath. His Adam's apple bobbed as he swallowed. He seemed to be holding his breath and his face was still and intent, as it always was when he listened to any story of injustice.

'We have no way of knowing the location of the SAS hostages,' Hector said. 'The Congo rainforest is vast – the second largest in the world after the Amazon. It covers an area of 1.5 million square miles. It's thick, impenetrable and teeming with life, most of it unfriendly to humans. We can't possibly know where our SAS guys are. Juwani's people have got an advantage over us there, so we're going to have to think a little smarter.' He looked at each of them in turn. 'You're going to have to think a little smarter,' he said.

Think a little smarter. Sami had repeated those words to himself more times than he could count over the past few days. They had been his mantra as the cadets travelled by helicopter from their headquarters, Valley House in the Scottish highlands. He had repeated it to himself as they flew from London to Kinshasa, the capital of the DRC.

As he learned about Oscar Juwani, and the atrocities he committed against children as young as ten, Sami became more determined to stop his wickedness. Sami had grown up on the war-torn streets of Syria. He had seen children suffer. So, yes, he was prepared to think a little smarter.

The loadie held up a finger.

One minute until the drop.

Unconsciously, Sami felt for the cord attaching his parachute rig to the static line apparatus. He was ready to jump. More than ready. He glanced over his shoulder. Lili stood close behind. Her expression was as sharp as ever. Sami thought back to the briefing – and the way Lili had second-guessed the Watchers' plan before they could relay it to the cadets.

'So if we can't find the SAS team,' Hector said, 'we only have one real option. We need Juwani's people to lead them to us.'

'You want to use us as bait,' Lili said.

'Bait's not the word I'd use,' Hector said, sounding a little uncomfortable.

'What word would you use? I speak four languages, Hector. I can't think of a better word in any of them.'

Hector had no reply. 'We know roughly the area in which Juwani's people are operating. They go from village to village, press-ganging children into joining them. Sometimes they persuade the kids that it would be good for them and they'll be able to send money back to their families. Sometimes they just abduct them. Your aim is to insert yourself into one of these villages – it's called Chakunda – and wait for the press gangs to arrive. When they do, let yourself be recruited or abducted. We reckon you will be taken into the rainforest to Juwani's stronghold, where the SAS team are almost certainly being held. Once you're there, you will activate a high-powered GPS personal locator beacon, or PLB, hidden inside this watch.' He held up a stainless-steel watch. 'These are normally used by explorers and climbers to send an emergency signal if they get into trouble. But this must only be activated when you are in the vicinity of the captured SAS team. As soon we receive the signal, a full SAS squadron led by me, Woody and Angel will mount an immediate rescue mission. We'll get the SAS hostages – and you – out of there.'

'You make it sound so easy,' Abby said.

'Then let me clarify,' Hector said. 'The jungle can be one of the most hostile environments for humans to operate in. The people whose ranks you are infiltrating are violent, immoral and merciless. This isn't just your most dangerous operation yet, it could be the riskiest mission the Special Forces Cadets have ever undertaken.'

Woody and Angel, who had been SFCs in their youth, nodded their agreement.

'The clock is ticking. The longer we delay, the smaller

our guys' chance of survival. So get ready to move. Your operation has started.'

Thirty seconds until the jump.

The cadets shuffled towards the tailgate. It was an awkward manoeuvre because of the rucksacks strapped to their legs. The light behind the loadmaster still glowed red. Lili felt sweat trickle down the nape of her neck. The nagging throb of anxiety that had been her constant companion since she'd understood the nature of this mission grew more intense. She had a bad feeling about it. A feeling that some of them, maybe all of them, wouldn't be coming back.

That's stupid, she told herself. She glanced across at her fellow cadets. Sami: so slight and quiet, yet so keen and skilled. Abby: quick of thought and tougher than she looked, which was saying something. Lukas: surly, and obviously more scared than he wanted to let on, but also a reassuring presence. And Max: quiet, kind, intelligent Max. The unspoken leader of their little group. If anyone could pull this off, they could.

The light turned green. The loadmaster lowered his arm.

'Here comes the bait, Oscar Juwani,' Lili muttered as Max hurled himself from the aircraft. Did Lukas hesitate before he followed? No, he was out. Then Abby and Sami in quick succession. Lili shuffled to the edge of the tailgate and felt the loadmaster's hand on her shoulder.

Was she pushed or did she jump? She didn't quite know. But suddenly she was in the air, the wind rushing in her ears. The parachute opened above her and she floated gently towards the treetops.

2

Treejumping

By the time Max's parachute opened, the roar of the Herc's engines had faded.

Over the past several weeks, the cadets had undergone extensive parachute training. An instructor had come up from No. 1 Parachute Training School in Brize Norton. He had taken them to an old barn a couple of miles from Valley House which had been kitted out for the express purpose of teaching the cadets how to jump out of an aircraft. They had begun by learning the parachute landing fall, or PLF. The instructor had laid crash mats on the ground and explained that, in order to carry out a parachute descent without injury and so be ready for combat on insertion, it was crucial that they mastered the PLF. The cadets had spent many hours jumping onto the mats and perfecting the art of landing: feet together, then their calves hitting the ground, then their thighs, then their back, and rolling over, tightly and securely, onto their opposite side, their chin on their chest.

Once they'd bossed the PLF, the instructor had

suspended the cadets from a rig in the ceiling to teach them their emergency drills: how to respond instantly to a malfunction, how to deploy their emergency chute and how to tug on the suspension lines to turn the parachute. Once they were conversant with the drills, the cadets had been taken to a nearby airfield and into an aircraft to perform some side-door exits. They had carried out seven daytime drops and one by night. Max found he had a talent for it. He received no words of encouragement from Hector, of course, who watched the proceedings with a critical scowl. But Woody had taken him to one side after the night drop. 'Your dad was a fine parachutist,' he had said. 'Looks like you inherited his talent.'

Max had given him a grateful look. That quiet word of encouragement meant a great deal to him. Max's father had founded the SFCs, and in a weird kind of way Max felt closer to his father, learning the same skills as he had learned. It was the only real link Max felt they shared.

Learning the techniques involved in treejumping, however, had been a more last-minute operation. Hours before their deployment, the cadets had found themselves hanging from a jumping tower, learning how to extract and fit lanyards to their harnesses and how to abseil down to the ground. Max had those techniques fixed firmly in his mind as he floated towards the jungle canopy, but he was painfully aware that his treejumping skills had been learned in theory rather than in practice.

At first, the canopy was a blanket of green. Now he could see the irregular shapes of individual trees. His instinct was to head for a gap between two trees, but that could be fatal: he needed his parachute rig to get tangled in the branches. So he selected a tree and pulled his suspension lines to drift towards it. Out of the corner of his eye he could just see Lukas ahead and to his left, then he pulled his attention back to his landing zone. He hunched up into a fetal position, covering his head and face with his arms, protecting his vital organs and making himself as small as possible. He prayed that his heavily padded jump suit would protect him from the impact because he was going to hit the treeline in three . . .

Two . . .

One . . .

He plunged into the jungle. Sharp branches poked at him, making him wince. His ears were filled with the rustling sound of his body falling through the foliage. He realised it was suddenly much darker: what light the canopy let through came only in narrow beams, shooting laser-like down to the forest floor.

There was a shocking jolt as his parachute rig became tangled in the branches. The parachute rig harness dug deeply into his body. He gasped. He was hanging in mid-air, swinging gently like a pendulum, at least the height of a house from the ground. His heart was thumping, his breathing heavy. At first, these were the only sounds he could hear. But as the seconds passed, his awareness spread like ripples on a pond. He could hear monkeys shrieking and scampering through the trees. Birds whose call he had never before heard chirruped deafeningly all around. Something slithered on a branch above him, chilling Max's blood. The forest was a riot of sounds. His own heartbeat and breathing were the ones that didn't belong there. That frightening thought was like a punch in the stomach.

He peered through the trees, trying to catch sight of the other cadets. Nothing, and he knew better than to call to them and give away his position to anyone who might be in the vicinity. No – his priority was to get to the ground. He had to work fast. He had no idea how securely he was hanging from the tree. He needed to rope up before his parachute rig slipped. From the pouch on his chest he removed the shorter rope. It was only about two metres long and had a metal carabiner at one end. He searched for a branch to fix himself to. There was nothing in reach. The sturdiest and closest was more than an arm's length away. He would have to swing towards it. He shifted his weight gingerly, first left, then right, careful not to make any sudden movements that might dislodge his rig from the foliage above. Stretching out his right arm, he clawed for the branch. He missed it the first time, but managed to hook his arm over it on his second attempt. He held it tightly while he wrapped the short rope around it, looping the leading end through the carabiner and quickly clipping it to his abseiling harness.

No longer at the mercy of his parachute rig, he turned his attention to the second rope. This also had a carabiner at one end. He looped it around the branch and fed the leading end through the carabiner as he had before, so that the rope was secure. He then fed the rope through the figure-of-eight descender that was clipped to his abseiling harness. He let the rest of the rope fall and was pleased to see that it reached the ground.

He was sweating heavily, but he couldn't lose his concentration. He unclipped his parachute harness and wriggled out of it, leaving it hanging from the tree. Then he undid his shorter safety rope. Attached only by his abseiling harness, he carefully lowered himself as he had been taught by the Watchers back at Valley House.

It was good to be on solid ground. But he instantly realised that the jungle was a harsh place to operate. The earth was mossy and damp underfoot. The air was hot, humid and difficult to breathe. A cloud of insects buzzed around his head. Absentmindedly, he slapped at his face with one hand as he removed his abseiling harness with the other. He unstrapped his rucksack from his legs. Only then did he try to peer through the jungle. Here on the ground the visibility was even worse: the undergrowth was thick and he did not have the advantage of height he had had in the tree. The strange, haunting sounds of the forest continued in his ears, making him feel dangerously alone. The sooner he made contact with the others, the better. He suppressed his instinct to move through the forest and find them. They had a plan: the others were to come to him. He whistled loudly. The chirruping of the jungle birds quietened at this strange new sound, then returned to its usual volume. There was another whistle in the distance: Lukas, most likely, confirming that he'd heard Max and making contact with the others.

Two minutes later, Max whistled again. This time he heard three whistles in response, much closer. He didn't need to whistle a third time. He saw movement in the foliage twenty paces to his nine o'clock. Quietly, Lukas emerged, followed by the others.

The team had barely been in the jungle for fifteen minutes and already it was getting to them. Their faces were moist from the humidity, and dirty. They each had their own personal cloud of insects. Sami and Abby had already been bitten. Lili had grazed her cheek during the insertion, though it didn't seem to bother her. Of all of them, however, Lukas looked the most uncomfortable. Max had the feeling this strange environment was freaking him out more than the others. His eyes darted from left to right and his frown was even more pronounced than usual.

Nobody spoke. There was no need. The Watchers had drilled them well and they knew what to do. Each cadet removed their helmet and padded jump suit. Underneath, they wore sturdy hiking gear: tough, quick-drying trousers and shirts. Wide-brimmed hats and mosquito head nets. Weathered Gore-Tex boots. Snake gaiters covering their lower legs to protect them from snake bites. Their clothes were not military. They had no camouflage gear or operational apparatus. They had no GPS or radios, because that wouldn't fit with their cover story. There was only one exception to that rule. Max felt in the left-hand chest pocket of his shirt. Inside was something circular and hard. It was his Special Forces Cadets challenge coin, which he had secretly sewn into the fabric of his shirt. Each of the cadets had been awarded one of these the day they passed selection. The Watchers were convinced that nobody they were likely to encounter would know what they were, even if they found them. But if ever the cadets needed to identify themselves to the authorities, they would use the challenge coins. Until that happened, the coins were to be kept hidden.

Max let his fingers fall and examined his friends. They looked suitably dirty and bedraggled. All their clothes had been pre-scuffed, dirtied and ripped in places, to make it look as if they had been trekking through the forest for some time. Days, at least. Their cover story, should anybody ask, was simple: they had been travelling through the jungle with an environmental group doing research into Congolese gorillas and had become separated from their friends. They would claim that they had survived their harsh surroundings for two days and two nights. Their gear needed to tell the same story.

So did their skin. Max grabbed a clump of moss from the forest floor and rubbed it into his face before putting on his mosquito head net. While the others were preparing themselves in the same way, he checked his watch.

Like the rest of the cadets' gear, Max's watch was scuffed and weathered. It looked quite ordinary, though perhaps a little chunkier than most watches. There was a good reason for that. This was the personal locator beacon. As soon as the cadets had located the missing SAS team, it was Max's responsibility to activate the beacon. To do this, he had to pull the dial on the side of the watch. This would extend a long, flexible antenna and send a GPS signal strong enough to penetrate the jungle canopy, if necessary.

'Maybe you should keep it in your rucksack,' Lili said quietly. 'You know, out of sight.'

'I dunno,' Max said. 'I feel kind of safer with it round my wrist where I can see it. If we lose this thing, we're in trouble.'

Max pulled the sleeve of his shirt over his watch and opened up the battered North Face rucksack at his feet.

It was double-lined with sturdy plastic liners to keep the contents dry. He fished out a sharp, broad-bladed knife, carefully stowed in a sturdy sheath. He took it out and examined the blade – one edge smooth, the other serrated – before re-sheathing it and hanging it from his leather belt. Then he turned to Sami.

His Syrian friend had a button compass in his right hand and was orientating himself. 'Hector told us that the village we're to head for is approximately two miles north-west of our landing zone,' he reminded them. He pointed into the forest. 'That way,' he said.

The jungle was identical in every direction. North-west was as thick and impenetrable as every other bearing. They had no alternative; they had to hack their way through the undergrowth. It would be exhausting, energy-sapping work. To travel two miles in such conditions would take the better part of the day.

'Everybody ready?' Max asked his friends. They left their jump suits in a pile on the ground. Max's parachute was still suspended from the canopy. The cadets all had their rucksacks strapped to their backs, their mosquito head nets covering their faces and their knives in their hands or hanging from their belts.

'Ready,' they said in unison.

'Then let's get moving,' Max said.

'And try not to step on a mamba,' Abby said lightly.

'You had to say it, didn't you?' Max muttered.

'Snakes not your thing, Max?'

'No,' Max said. 'They're really not.'

'You probably shouldn't have come to the jungle, then. Apparently they quite like it here. Shall we go?'

3

Grub

Moving through the jungle was hard work. Sami took the lead, following the north-westerly bearing he had established. With one hand, he hacked his way through the thick, tough greenery. With the other, he held a sturdy stick to prod the ground and warn off any hidden snakes. Nobody could keep that up for long. After twenty minutes Sami was drenched with sweat and his arms were growing weak. Max, just behind him, whispered his name. Sami stopped. His face was sodden under his mosquito net.

'Let me go first for a bit,' Max said.

Sami didn't argue. They swapped places, double-checked their bearings and Max continued to hack through the forest. He was soaked in sweat within two minutes, the moisture trickling into his eyes half blinding him. Within ten, his arms ached and his muscles burned. His shirt was torn in several places and he had tiny cuts all over his hand. He was vaguely aware that the monkeys screeching in the canopy overhead had grown louder. He wondered if groups of them were following the cadets.

He decided not to worry about that. He had to focus on hacking his way through the jungle . . .

'*Max!*' Sami shouted. '*Watch out!*'

Max froze. What was Sami warning him about? A snake? Some other creature? He felt himself being yanked backwards, and almost toppled. A second later, a thick dead branch crashed to the ground, landing at Max's feet. Max swore under his breath, his heart racing. Above him, the canopy was alive with movement: monkeys swarmed through the treetops, hundreds of them. Had they mischievously thrown the branch to the ground, or had their movement simply dislodged it? It didn't much matter either way. If Sami hadn't been so quick, that branch would have hit Max. It could have killed him.

The cadets stood in stunned silence. 'I'm thinking,' Abby said, slightly out of breath, 'that from now on we look *up* as well as *forward*.'

'This is ridiculous,' Lili said. Her voice was a little more high-pitched than usual. 'How do we even know we're going in the right direction? Vaguely heading north-west is hardly reliable.'

Nobody had an answer to that. They stood there without speaking as the noises of the jungle started to close in on them.

'What's that?' Lili whispered.

Max listened hard. There was a distant sound of running water. He grinned at Lili.

'What is it?' Lukas demanded with a frown.

'Water,' Max said. 'And in the jungle, water leads to civilisation. Chakunda's the only village round here, right? My bet is the water leads there. We need to find it.'

Lukas seemed unable to find a problem with that. He drew himself up to his full height and breathed deeply, as if filling himself with confidence. 'My turn to lead,' he said.

The water was off to their right. They moved more slowly now that they had to check for falling debris and listen for the stream, but gradually the sound grew louder. Within ten minutes they had found a stream, narrow enough to jump over. It was murky but fast-flowing and travelled in a straight line. Abby eyed it uncertainly. 'Crocodiles?' she said.

'I don't think so,' Max said. 'It's just a tiny stream, not a river. I don't think this is their habitat.'

'Wild animals will come here though,' Lili said. 'To drink. We must be watchful.'

The others nodded their agreement.

There was a rough trail by the stream. Max thought it had been made by animals, rather than humans. He saw teeth marks on the foliage and clumps of fur caught on branches. Trees overhung the stream, and the ground was knotted with roots. Despite that, the going was easier here, even though they still had to step carefully, keep looking up, and occasionally hack their way through thickets and patches of impenetrable jungle.

'Hey, Lili?' Max said after they had been going for ten minutes. He was at the back of the line and she was just ahead of him.

'Uh-huh?' she said.

'Does Lukas seem okay to you?'

She stopped and turned. Her face, shaded by her net, was drenched in sweat and humidity. 'Now you mention it,' she said, 'he's been in a strange mood ever since we were briefed on this mission. Back at Valley House I offered him my pudding after dinner. He turned it down.' She frowned. 'Lukas *never* turns down pudding.'

'It's more than that,' Max said, a little irritated that Lili didn't seem to be taking him seriously. 'It's like he's not part of the team any more. Like he doesn't want to be here.'

Lili gave Max a 'do *you* really want to be here?' look.

'You know what I mean,' Max said. 'It's just . . . he's not himself.'

'I'm sure he's fine. We can't always bring our A game, you know.'

'Yeah, maybe,' Max said. He couldn't help thinking that if ever there *was* a time to bring your A game, this was it.

'We'd better keep going,' Lili said. 'The others are way ahead.'

Morning turned to afternoon. The stream meandered only occasionally and the cadets stuck with it, rather than trying to keep going in a straight line and lose their water source. They grew hungry. As they rested for a few minutes, splashing their faces with water from the stream, Abby started poking around beneath a fallen log. 'Hey, Abby,' Max said, 'careful. You know snakes hide under logs, right?'

'No snakes here, Maxy,' she said. She turned and held up something between her thumb and forefinger. It was a pale cream colour, about two inches long and almost as fat. It squirmed and wriggled in Abby's grasp. 'Palm grub,' she announced. 'Anybody else peckish?'

The cadets stared at her in horror.

'What?' she said defensively. 'It's good food, isn't it? Lots of protein.'

'That's gross,' Lukas said.

'Put it down, Abby,' Lili said. 'We're not starving yet.'

'Speak for yourself, sister.'

'Just put it down. That thing could make you really ill.'

Rather regretfully, Abby put the grub back down in the shade of the log. Something in the vegetation caught Max's eye. He parted the foliage and reached for one of the round green fruits he had seen hanging from a tree. He plucked it. 'Hey, Abby,' he said. 'Catch!' He threw the fruit at her. Abby's reflexes were fast and she caught it with ease. 'It's a guava,' Max said.

'And what do I do with a guava?'

'What do you think? You eat it.'

'Maxy, baby, I could kiss you.'

'How about you save the kisses and show me your gratitude by not calling me Maxy baby?'

'Deal,' Abby said, and bit into the fruit. 'Well, it's no Snickers,' she said through a mouthful of guava, 'but it'll do.'

Max plucked some more guavas and threw them to the other cadets. They ate gratefully. Only Lukas seemed unimpressed. He threw his guava into the stream without a word. Lili caught Max's eye as if to say, *maybe you were right*. Lukas reached into his pocket and pulled out a clear Ziploc bag. Was it really filled with . . .

'Biscuits?' Abby said incredulously. 'You had biscuits all this time?'

Lukas shrugged. 'I came prepared,' he said. Rather reluctantly, he held the bag out to the cadets.

'What?' Abby said. 'Boring old biscuits when we've got these delicious . . . What did you say they were, Max?'

The cadets laughed, all except Lukas, who scowled at them, crammed a biscuit in his mouth and shoved the bag back into his pocket.

Minutes later they were on the move again. They were silent as they struggled through their unfamiliar surroundings. None of them said what Max suspected they were all thinking: that if this strategy of following the stream was wrong, they were hopelessly lost. That would mean activating the personal locator beacon in his watch before the mission had even properly started. Max was just imagining Hector's disapproving words and Woody and Angel's disappointed faces, when he noticed that the foliage was thinning out. The stream was wider here, though the canopy was thicker. Abby, who was leading, halted. 'What's that smell?' she said.

Everyone stopped. Max sniffed. No doubt about it: woodsmoke tinged the air. 'Either the jungle's on fire,' he said, 'or that's a fire from the village. Come on, we're getting close.'

4

Roland

The village of Chakunda lay in a wide clearing where the jungle trees had been felled and the vegetation cut away. But as the cadets surveyed it from behind the treeline, Max could almost feel the jungle straining at the perimeter of the village, like a hostile army desperate to retake open ground.

It looked like a village from another time. Huts, perhaps fifty of them, were dotted around. They were constructed from slim tree trunks with rush roofs. In the centre of the village was a clearing where a pit fire billowed smoke into the air. There were other small fires outside some of the huts, over which the village women, dressed in colourful skirts and tops with elaborate headscarves, were cooking food.

The men had congregated in the central clearing. Most wore jeans and faded tops. One of them was in an old Manchester United shirt. There were perhaps thirty of them, and there was something strange about their demeanour. None of them seemed to be speaking. Each man stood alone, peering away from the village as if trying to see into the surrounding jungle.

Nine or ten children played in the dust not far from where the cadets stood, watching, but there was something listless about them.

There were no vehicles, of course, because there were no roads. A couple of wheelbarrows leaned against a nearby hut. A few rusted oil drums lay on their sides here and there. This was obviously a poor place, without electricity or running water or any modern conveniences. It was also, he had the impression, waiting for something bad to happen.

'Do we just walk in?' Sami said.

'I don't see that we have much choice,' Max said. 'But don't expect a warm welcome.'

Their intention was to present themselves as lost travellers, bedraggled, hungry and scared. It didn't take much acting. As they emerged gingerly from behind the treeline, the children immediately stopped their game and stared silently at the little group of newcomers. Lukas took the lead. His black skin was less alien to the villagers, but Max thought that for some reason the children seemed more scared of him than of the rest of them.

The cadets filed into the centre of the village. Out of the corner of his eye, Max saw some of the women leave their cooking fires and hurry towards the children, scooping them up in their arms or ushering them into the huts. The men in the central clearing turned to face them, squaring their shoulders as if preparing for a fight. A few of them held rocks. But there was nothing confident or aggressive about them. They seemed as scared as the women and children, even if they were trying to hide it.

Silence fell over the village. The cadets stood in a line. The women and children had disappeared into the huts and the men had formed a huddle. It suddenly dawned on Max that the villagers might think the cadets were Oscar Juwani's people. If so, he thought, their tactics were all wrong. They shouldn't be bunched up in a group like that, an easy target for anybody with an automatic weapon. They should be spread out, ready to act. Even as he thought this, he had a mental image of the Watchers nodding their approval at his tactical thinking. When had he started seeing the world like that? he wondered.

Lili stepped forward. 'Does anybody speak English?' she called in a clear, confident voice.

The men muttered and shook their heads. Unsurprisingly, it seemed that nobody did. Then a figure appeared from behind a nearby hut. He was no older than the cadets, and skinny. His hair was wiry and scruffy and his clothes hung off him. He seemed as nervous as the rest of the villagers.

'I speak English,' he said, biting his lower lip. 'Who are you?'

Lili glanced at the others. 'We're lost,' she said.

'You are not . . . You are not here to attack us?'

'What? No, of course not. We've been walking through the jungle for two days. We need somewhere to rest. C-could you help us? Please?'

The young man frowned. 'You should leave,' he said. 'It is more dangerous here than in the forest. Leave! Go!'

He turned his back on them, hurried over to the men and started talking to them in their own language. Max assumed that this was Lingala, but there were so many different languages spoken in the DRC that he couldn't be sure.

'Well, I'd say you were right about the warm welcome,' Abby drawled. 'What now?'

Max removed his backpack and fished around in one of the outer pockets, where he had stashed a bundle of Congolese francs. He peeled off several notes and led the cadets towards the central clearing, holding up the money. 'We can pay,' he called. 'We only need a little food and water, and some help getting home.'

The money instantly grabbed the villagers' attention. They were suddenly less hostile. One of the older men said something to the boy who spoke English, and pushed him back towards the cadets. Max held out his hand. 'I'm Max,' he said. 'This is Lukas, Abby, Sami, Lili. What's your name?'

'Roland,' the boy said.

'How come you speak such good English?'

Roland glanced towards the huts. 'An English person came here once. A missionary. He taught me his language.' He frowned. 'But then he disappeared. I think they killed him.'

'Who?'

Roland shook his head. 'It doesn't matter.'

Max let it go. 'Here,' he said, and handed over the money. Roland gave it to the older man, then turned back to Max. 'Why are you here?' he said.

'We were on a trip, searching for gorillas.'

'Why would you *search* for gorillas? What else are you *searching* for? Snakes? Don't you know how dangerous they are?'

'Sure, but we were with experts. We got separated from them somehow – I don't know how.'

Roland's expression darkened. 'Gorillas are not the most dangerous creatures in this jungle, I suppose,' he said, and glanced nervously towards the treeline.

'What do you mean?'

The boy sniffed. 'Come with me,' he said. 'I have some water you can drink.'

The cadets followed Roland to his hut. The other villagers seemed to have lost interest in them. The women had re-emerged and were tending their fires. The men were counting out the notes Max had given them. Only the children paid them any attention. They followed.

Roland said something sharply to them, but he had a twinkle in his eye and Max could tell he didn't mean it. The kids could tell that too: they giggled and continued to follow.

Roland fetched a wooden jug of water and several wooden bowls from his hut. The cadets drank gratefully, then sat on the ground outside at Roland's insistence. A boy no older than five threw himself onto Lukas's back. Lukas's frown instantly melted into a grin, and he tickled the kid mercilessly. The others smiled to see it. When the kid had wriggled out of Lukas's grasp, Roland spoke to the children again. This time they took him more seriously, and left him and the cadets to talk.

'I mean it,' Roland said. 'You would be better not to stay here. You would be better to take your chances in the jungle. There are bad people in the area. It is only a matter of time before they arrive here. They have been seen nearby. When they come . . .' Roland shuddered and glanced in the direction of the children.

'What?' Abby said.

'Have you heard of Oscar Juwani?'

'No,' Abby lied. The cadets shook their heads.

'Oscar Juwani is the worst man in the world,' Roland said. 'I have seen him. To meet him is to meet the Devil.'

Max found he was holding his breath.

'Why?' Abby asked.

'His face is scarred from fighting,' Roland said. 'One

of his eyes is the colour of milk. Nobody knows if he can see out of it or not. But that's not what makes him evil. What he *does* makes him evil.' He lowered his voice. 'He takes children and young people. Their families never see them again. They are forced to do terrible things.'

'What sort of things?' Sami said. His jaw was set.

'Things they could never admit to. Things that bind them to Oscar Juwani for life. They become his soldiers and his worshippers. He sees himself as a god, and the children as his disciples.'

'How come you met him?' Max asked.

'It doesn't matter,' Roland said. 'All that matters is that we know Oscar Juwani's people are close. They have been seen in the forest. Yesterday word reached us that they had attacked a village a day's walk from here. They murdered many adults and stole the young people. They will come here next, and when they do . . .' He waved an arm. 'Many of us have fled. Those who have remained are not strong enough to fight them.'

'Why didn't you leave?' Lukas asked.

'Where would I go? My friends, please, leave. Oscar Juwani would like to catch you. Get away from here before it's too late.'

The cadets sat in silence. Roland's impassioned plea had chilled Max. Leaving, however, was not an option. He shook his head. 'The group we were with will try to find us in villages like this one. We can't keep moving around. We have to stay put, or we'll never get home.' He gave Roland an unconvincing smile. 'I'm sure it will be fine,' he said.

Roland gave a 'don't blame me if it goes wrong' shrug. 'You may use my hut,' he said. 'I will find you all something to eat. We don't have much, but what we do have, we will share.' He stood up, nodded to them and wandered off towards one of the other huts.

Abby exhaled heavily. 'Sounds like a charmer, this Oscar Juwani,' she said.

'Does it seem weird to you,' Lukas said, 'that Roland knows so much about him?'

'People talk,' Max said. But now that Lukas had planted the thought, he couldn't quite forget it. How had Roland seen Oscar Juwani face to face? What was the real reason he hadn't fled the village?

'Do you think Juwani's gang will really be here tonight?' Sami asked.

'The people are very nervous,' Lili said. 'Can't you feel it? They sense something is about to happen. Yes, I think it will be tonight.'

'If they try to kill someone,' Sami said, 'I will stop them.' He sounded determined.

'You know what Hector would say to that,' Max said.

'That we're not here to fight other people's battles?'

'Right.'

'Do you agree with him?' It was more a challenge than a question.

Max looked around. At the men, all on edge, waiting to protect their village. At the women, anxious about their children. And at the kids themselves, playing happily, as if there was nothing wrong.

'No,' Max said quietly. 'I don't.'

The food Roland provided – a kind of thick, grainy porridge – was plain but filling. The cadets kept to themselves and ate sitting in a circle as evening drew in. Night fell quickly, almost as if somebody had flicked a switch. The only light came from the central fire pit and the stars twinkling overhead. The sounds of the jungle grew quieter. From their position by Roland's hut, the cadets saw silhouettes of the adult villagers congregating around the fire. They spoke in low voices, but none of them invited the newcomers to join them.

The cadets themselves hardly spoke. This was their third mission together and Max was growing used to the period of quiet reflection that preceded potential danger. He was going over everything the Watchers had told him about this mission, going over all his training and skills. And he was remembering Roland's words: *Oscar Juwani is the worst man in the world. To meet him is to meet the Devil.*

Finally, the villagers fell silent and wandered to

their huts. A few of the men took up positions at the perimeter of the clearing, but they had no light and they weren't armed. Max checked his watch that hid the PLB. It was 23:00 exactly. At Roland's invitation they entered his tent. By the light of a smoky animal-fat candle, they saw that the interior was simple: a thin mattress, some cooking utensils and little else. The cadets each found themselves some floor space and, using their rucksacks as pillows, settled down for the night.

Max knew nobody was really asleep. The irregular breathing. The tossing and the turning. Although his limbs were tired, his mind was active and alert. He wished he could be at the perimeter of the village, watching. If – when – Oscar Juwani's gang arrived, he wanted to be in a position to help the villagers. But to do that would blow their cover. It was essential that the cadets appeared to be what they said they were: ordinary travellers, trying to get a night's sleep, caught in the wrong place at the wrong time.

The minutes ticked by. Midnight came and went. One o'clock. Two. A thick blanket of silence covered them, ruffled only by the occasional screech of an animal. Max realised his pulse was racing again, and he was drenched in sweat.

02:55. Max sat up. He'd heard something. It sounded like a monkey screech, but it was dark and the monkeys weren't active at night. Anyway, the sound wasn't quite right. It was more like a human, mimicking an animal.

The others sat up.

'They're coming,' Max whispered.

5

Sitting Ducks

It took all their restraint to stay still. There was another fake screech from the opposite side of the village. A call – and a response.

'The villagers should be in the jungle,' Abby whispered, 'waiting for the gang to enter the village. Then they could surround them and capture them.'

Max knew she was right, but these frightened people were not military tacticians. They were sitting ducks. And so were the cadets. They had to be.

Suddenly, there was a terrific noise – a hollering and screaming from all around. Horrific, bloodcurdling sounds. It was clearly intended to be frightening, and it was. Max tried to estimate how many voices there were. Twenty? Perhaps more. They sounded male, but not quite adult. After a few seconds the villagers also started to scream, and the night was filled with a deafening, panicky noise.

Roland, who had been sleeping by the entrance to the hut, rushed out. As he opened the door, Max caught a glimpse of the central fire pit. It was roaring, much higher than it had been earlier in the evening. He caught a stench of burning fuel, and realised the attackers must have doused it with petrol or some other fire-starter. Silhouettes rushed here and there in front of the flames. Then the door shut and the cadets were in darkness again.

'We can't just stay here,' Sami said. 'What if they hurt people?'

'We're here to be captured,' Lukas reminded him. 'We can't mess that up.'

Even as he spoke, a woman screamed. She sounded utterly desperate and terrified. Her scream was followed by another – a child this time.

'No,' Sami said. 'No way.' He stood up and burst out of the hut.

Max slapped his forehead and groaned. 'Sami, come back.' But he knew his friend wouldn't do that. He was just too good a person. He couldn't bear injustice, even if speaking out got him into trouble. That was why the cadets liked him so much, and they weren't going to abandon him. Already Abby and Lili were standing up to follow. Max did the same. So did Lukas, although he seemed a little more reluctant than the others.

Max could feel his heart pumping hard and a cold sweat on the nape of his neck. As they burst out of the hut, they were greeted by a scene of chaos. The village fire was still burning ferociously. It illuminated several young African men. Some had rifles slung across their chest. Others held rifles above their heads, screaming maniacally. It looked to Max like they were prepared to use those weapons.

Two of them were close. They wore red tops: one a T-shirt, one a thin jumper with holes in the sleeves. One man stood behind a woman from the village, clutching her hair in one hand. His other hand held a knife to her throat. The woman was screaming desperately but didn't dare move. The second man stood behind a child who couldn't have been more than eight years old. The boy was kneeling and the young man held a rifle to the back of his skull. The kid's face was wet with tears and his body was shuddering. The gunman's face was as contorted with rage as his friend's. He looked like he was going to shoot the boy.

'Don't do it!' Max screamed.

His words were drowned out by a sudden burst of automatic gunfire elsewhere in the village. The screaming and general chaos increased and the sound seemed to fuel the gunman's madness. Max could tell that he was going to shoot the kid any second. He took a step forward, but there was nothing he could do. The gunman squeezed the trigger.

There was a click.

'Stoppage,' Sami hissed. As the gunman stared, frustrated, at his weapon, Sami dived over the kneeling boy at the gunman, knocking him to the ground. At the same time, Abby and Lili hurled themselves towards the guy with the knife. The gunman's problem with his weapon had clearly distracted his mate, who had lowered the knife a little as he peered over the woman's shoulder to see what was happening.

Big mistake.

If the gang were like wild dogs, Abby and Lili were highly skilled birds of prey. They almost seemed to fly towards the knife man. Lili grabbed his knife arm and yanked it back sharply. There was a sickening crack. Abby pushed the woman roughly away from the man then brought her fist down hard on the young man's neck, right on his carotid artery. He collapsed, unconscious, to the ground.

The kid scurried to his mum while Sami wrestled with the gunman. Max ran to help him. As Sami pinned the young man's arms to the ground, Max seized his rifle. He made it safe before removing the clip, throwing the neutered weapon into Roland's hut and scattering the rounds on the ground. By this time, Sami had also delivered a well-placed blow to the gunman's neck. He lay, unconscious, on the ground.

Sami sprang to his feet. The woman and her frightened son disappeared into the melee of noisy, frightened villagers. The cadets looked at the motionless figures on the ground, then at each other. Lukas was scowling. 'You shouldn't have done that,' he hissed. 'You'll blow our cover.'

'They were going to kill that boy,' Sami retorted, not bothering to keep his voice down. 'What were we supposed to do? Watch?'

Lukas couldn't answer. There was another burst of automatic fire and a sudden clamour of voices. There was shouting, punctuated with bursts from a rifle. The villagers congregated in a huddle by the central fire pit. Many were holding children. Some were kneeling. Armed gang members swarmed around them, yelling and making aggressive motions with their weapons. Max tried to pick out Roland, but couldn't among the terrified throng of villagers. Suddenly he became aware that he and the other cadets stood apart from the villagers. 'We should get away from these two,' he said, pointing at the unconscious figures on the ground. Even as the others nodded in agreement, however, he felt a strange prickling sensation down his spine. Were they being watched?

He turned. There, just a few paces away, stood a small group of young men. Armed.

There were five, but all Max's attention was on one of them. He stood at the front of the little group, dwarfing them. It was hard to gauge his age, but he had downy hair on his face, which made Max think he was a teenager, despite his height. His hair was closely cropped, apart from a mane down the middle of his scalp, tied tightly in a

44

ponytail. He wore trousers and a rough black waistcoat – Max noticed that all his companions wore black tops too – with a bandolier of ammunition slung across his chest. His arms twitched and rippled with muscle. He was carrying a submachine gun in his right hand. It was almost an extension of his arm. But worse than his size, or the weapon, were his eyes. They reflected the flames at the centre of the village, but they looked strangely hollow and dead. They were the eyes, Max thought, of a person for whom killing was commonplace.

The man glanced at his two comrades lying unconscious on the ground. His lip curled with disdain. He gave a short command that Max did not understand. Two of his companions swaggered past the cadets to the unconscious bodies and dragged them towards the fire. The tall guy asked the cadets a question in an unpleasant, rasping voice.

The cadets glanced sidelong at each other. It was Abby who spoke up. 'We're not from here,' she said. 'We got lost and . . .' Uncharacteristically, her voice petered out.

The tall guy laughed: a humourless bark. He stepped towards them and continued to speak. Max couldn't understand a word, even though he found himself focusing hard. The panicked shouts of the villagers receded in his head. He knew he could do nothing for them. He could also tell that these young men in their black tops and their high-spec weapons were not like the two guys the cadets had disarmed minutes earlier. They carried themselves more confidently. And bubbling under the surface was the threat of even more violence.

The cadets didn't move. The tall guy strolled among them. When he reached Lukas, the only one of the cadets who was physically a match for him, he stopped. Almost chest to chest with him, the tall guy said one word. His three companions joined him. They grabbed Lukas's wrists and bound them tightly behind his back with cable ties. One of them retrieved a hood from a shoulder bag and pulled it over Lukas's head. Lukas made no attempt to struggle, though it was everything Max could do to stop himself from helping his mate.

Abby was next. 'You sure know how to treat a girl,' she said as they bound and hooded her. They moved on to Sami and Lili, who accepted their fate in silence. Finally the tall guy approached Max. He was a head taller than him. As he drew closer, the stench of stale sweat and alcohol hit Max's nostrils. The guy whispered something. When Max felt his wrists being grabbed and tightly tied behind his back, he forced himself not to resist. The hood, when it was pulled over his head, was uncomfortably rough and smelled foul. Max wanted to gag. He also wanted to run. But even if that had been part of their plan, fear would have kept him planted there. He seemed to have lost all the strength in his limbs.

The frightened noises of the villagers were muffled, their screams fewer. But Max heard four single shots.

They sounded nearby, and so loud that they seemed to go through his body. For a sickening moment, Max thought his friends had been shot. No, he told himself quickly. If they were going to kill us, they wouldn't have bothered with the ties and the hoods. As the gunshots faded away, however, he heard a dreadful moan of despair. *Someone had just been killed.* The image of the little kid with the gun to his head jumped into his mind, and he felt sick.

But that didn't last for long. He felt something hard and unyielding crack into his skull. The world spun. Nausea overwhelmed him, and he blacked out.

6

Blackshirts

The next few hours passed in a blur.

When Max woke, he still wore the hood and his wrists were still tied. There was a crushing ache in his skull, and he was overwhelmed with nausea. It was all he could do to stop himself vomiting. Rough hands pulled him to his feet and dragged him about. Voices barked and hissed. He could smell smoke and hear the intense crackle of flames. Was the village burning? Occasionally he tripped and fell to his knees, but was quickly pulled up again and pushed forward. He had no idea where they were heading. He listened hard for the voices of his fellow cadets but couldn't hear them. Were they still with him? Were they still alive? He couldn't tell.

He felt a rope being looped around his neck, as if he was a dog on a leash. Somebody pulled him and he staggered. The rope choked him. The sound of flames and frightened villagers faded away. Max could feel foliage brushing against him. He realised he no longer had his rucksack, and was glad he hadn't taken Lili's advice about stowing his watch in there. Even through his hood, he could sense the thick humidity of the jungle. He knew he was being moved away from the village, but didn't know where to or in which direction. His fingers were swollen because of the tight cable ties that bound his wrists, but he managed to feel for his watch. It was some comfort to find it there, but his stomach churned with anxiety. Their abductors were more violent than he had ever imagined them being. They were killers, and Max sensed that they had a taste for it. Maybe he should activate the PLB immediately? This had gone much worse than any of them had expected. He restrained himself, but his fingers still felt for the watch.

Time passed. He didn't know how long, but the jungle sounds around him grew louder, so Max knew dawn must be arriving. Monkeys screeched. Birds called. A riot of sound that reminded him of the seething mass of life all around him.

His neck was rubbed raw by the rope. Suddenly, the person leading him yanked it sharply and barked a single word. Max took it as an instruction to stop. Rough hands removed his hood. He blinked as light stabbed his eyes.

Where was he? He tried to take in his surroundings. He was on a roughly hewn path. On either side were tall trees covered with spaghetti-like vines. He couldn't see far into the forest. Sunbeams cut through the canopy, illuminating clouds of water vapour and making the foliage glow a vivid emerald green. It was beautiful in its way, but there was nothing beautiful about the people around him.

The other cadets stood in a line in front of Max. They had also been led by ropes around their necks, each by one of the gang members. They looked dirty, exhausted and terrified, Lukas particularly. His left eye was cut and badly bruised, and he stared into the middle distance, as though unsure where he was or what he was doing. Behind Max were eight or nine villagers between the ages of about ten and sixteen. Unlike the cadets, they were not leashed. Instead, they were tied to each other by their wrists. They wore haunted, fearful expressions. Many of them had been crying. Max saw Roland at the end of the line, his head bowed.

And then, of course, there were the gang members. In Max's memory of the attack on the village, there had been hordes of them. In reality, there were no more than ten. Their weapons were lazily slung across their chests. Most of them also carried sturdy sticks. Max immediately saw why when one of them hit a younger child, who had just started to cry, hard around the knees. Only the cadets had a dedicated gang member leading them by the neck. The other abductors swaggered round their hostages, brandishing their sticks and their weapons, plainly enjoying their position of authority. At the head of the line stood the tall gang member with the scalped hair and mane. He eyed the cadets with suspicion. Max found himself wishing they hadn't drawn attention to themselves, but he supposed, with their mix of skin colours and nationalities, that it couldn't be helped.

The gang members removed the cadets' leashes and tied them, wordlessly, wrist to wrist, to the other hostages. Max found himself next to Roland. One of the gang members shouted something. The other hostages sat on the ground, so the cadets did the same. They sat in a group with Roland while one of the gang members walked among the hostages with a canteen of water, allowing them a sip. Max was desperate for water. His throat was dry and raw. But as the guy approached, Max realised he was one of the men they had knocked unconscious. He did not offer the cadets a drink.

Nobody could escape, even if they had wanted to. They were tied together. Anyway, where would they go? The ten gang members gathered at the head of the line where they shared some food among themselves. It gave the cadets the opportunity to regroup. 'I told you to leave,' Roland said bitterly. He was still hanging his head, as though trying to hide his face.

'You don't want them to recognise you,' Lili said quietly. 'Especially the tall guy.'

'His name is Babaka.'

'How do you know?'

Roland glanced left and right. He didn't reply. Max remembered that, from what he had said, Roland had

51

met Oscar Juwani before. 'Tell us,' he insisted. 'Maybe we can help you.'

Roland looked unwilling to speak. 'You can't help me,' he said, seeming to shrink into himself.

Max remembered something he had noticed during the attack. Babaka, and five of the gang members surrounding him, all wore black tops. They were not all the same style – some had T-shirts, some had waistcoats, others had shirts with collars. But they looked like a kind of uniform nevertheless. The four other gang members had mismatched red shirts. They congregated separately.

'Hey, Roland,' Max said quietly. 'What's with the shirts?'

Roland was obviously reluctant to speak.

'Come on, mate,' Max pressed him. 'We're scared. We want to know what's happening.'

'Oscar Juwani's hooligans are known as the Blackshirts,' Roland said. His voice was low, so the cadets had to strain to hear him. 'It is because the people closest to him, his inner circle, wear black shirts. They are the worst. They have killed many times, to show their loyalty to Oscar Juwani. He trusts them all. But there are also Redshirts and Blueshirts. The red shirts are worn by any boy or girl who has killed at least one person. They are less important than the Blackshirts and are not treated so well. But they are treated better than the Blueshirts.'

'Who are they?' Lili asked, an intent expression on her face.

'Everyone else. Us. We will be given blue shirts soon. Blueshirts are treated like slaves. They serve the Redshirts and the Blackshirts. They cook their food and dig their toilet pits. They are often beaten and go hungry. After a while, all the Blueshirts want to become Redshirts. It's either that or be a victim all their life. So they are willing to kill someone. And once they have killed one person, it is easy to kill a second. And then they are lost . . .'

An intense hatred was etched across Roland's face. He spoke as if the words tasted bad.

'How come you know so much?' Abby said, her voice gentle and persuasive.

'I was caught by Oscar Juwani's hooligans before,' he said. His voice cracked.

'When?' Sami asked.

'Two months ago. I was visiting my brother. Well, my half-brother. He lives in a nearby village. The hooligans came at night then too. It is their way. The Blackshirts and the Redshirts burned the village. Killed some of the elders. And they took the young people with them to Oscar Juwani's stronghold. Including my brother and me.'

One of the Blackshirts laughed loudly. The nearby Redshirts laughed along sycophantically.

'We tried to escape,' Roland continued more quietly. 'My brother and I. We made the gang think that we wanted to become Redshirts so they would not keep a close watch on us. Then one night we made our move. I think we would have got away, but as we entered the forest a Blueshirt saw us. He shouted out and the whole camp woke up. My brother and I ran. I managed to escape.' He drew a deep breath. 'My brother didn't.'

'What happened to him?' Sami asked.

Roland stared at the ground again. 'At first I did not know. News travels slowly here and people are scared to talk about what happens in Oscar Juwani's camp. But I found out later that my brother was killed by a Redshirt who wanted to become a Blackshirt. They shot him, then left his body in the jungle for the wild animals to take.'

The cadets stared at him in silent horror.

'I told you that Oscar Juwani is the worst man in the world. His Redshirts and his Blackshirts are almost as bad.'

'Maybe not,' Max said.

'What do you mean? A Redshirt killed my brother. I hate them.'

'But they would never have done it if Oscar Juwani hadn't captured them in the first place. It's what he does, isn't it? He takes ordinary young people and he forces them to do terrible things. He brainwashes them and changes who they are.' He nodded at one of the other prisoners, a boy of no more than ten. 'Look at him. If what you're saying is true, he's in for a rough time. It won't be long before he wants to be a Redshirt. And it could happen to any of us.'

'I hate them,' Roland repeated firmly.

'But –'

'Leave it, Max,' Abby said softly. 'Can't you see what the problem is here? Why do you think Roland's doing his best not to let his face be seen? What if one of these thugs recognises him as the boy who got away? It's obvious what they'll do to him.'

'And he can't stay anonymous for long,' Lili said. 'As soon as we get to Oscar Juwani's camp, someone is bound to recognise him. Maybe even Juwani himself. And then . . .'

'He will shoot Roland,' Sami said plainly.

'Shoot me?' Roland said. 'He won't shoot me. Oscar Juwani has other ways of dealing with people who make him angry.'

'Like what?' Lukas said.

Max wasn't sure Lukas had been following the conversation. It was the first time he had spoken since they stopped. When Roland hesitated, he looked angry. '*Like what?*' he repeated.

Roland didn't answer. Two of the Blackshirts were approaching, shouting orders. Roland quickly lowered his head again. 'They are telling us to be quiet,' he said. 'Don't talk to me again. It is too risky for me.' He fell silent.

But Max had a question. If Oscar Juwani's camp was such a dangerous place for Roland, why had he stayed in the village when he knew Juwani's men were on their way? Maybe, Max wondered, the cadets weren't the only people who wanted to be captured. He decided to keep an eye on Roland from now on.

7

The Clearing

One of the Redshirts shouted a harsh instruction. The abductees stood up and the cadets followed suit. But they didn't move. The tall Blackshirt was walking down the line of prisoners. He had a sturdy, solid stick, and held it as though he wanted to use it. Roland, next to Max, hung his head. Max wanted to hiss at him not to make it so obvious because he was likely to draw more attention to himself that way. But the Blackshirt was too close. In any case, it seemed that he was more interested in Lukas than in Roland.

The Blackshirt stopped right in front of Lukas.

Max had grown to know Lukas well. Sure, he was quiet and occasionally surly, but he could handle himself. Ever since they had parachuted into the Congo rainforest, however, he'd seemed less like himself. The strain of their mission seemed to be getting to him more than to the others. As the Blackshirt stood over him, he almost seemed to be in a trance.

The Blackshirt said something Max didn't understand.

Then he raised his stick. With a sudden, brutal movement he slammed it hard into Lukas's stomach.

'No!' Abby and Lili cried in unison. Lukas doubled over. He made a horrible rasping sound as he tried to inhale. The Blackshirt grinned and hit Lukas again in the ribs. He was like a pack animal proving his dominance. Maybe he knew that Lukas was the strongest of the hostages. Or maybe he sensed Lukas's mental weakness. Whatever the truth, Lukas didn't resist. He was coughing and wheezing in pain. Max remembered something Roland had said. *They are often beaten and go hungry. After a while, all the Blueshirts want to become Redshirts. It's either that or be a victim all their life.*

Right now, Lukas was more victim than Special Forces Cadet.

The Blackshirt raised his stick yet again. This time it was Max who shouted out. 'No! Leave him!'

The Blackshirt froze. He turned to Max. Then he lowered his stick and walked towards him.

Max steeled himself to receive a blow just like Lukas had. The Blackshirt rested the end of his cudgel against Max's cheek. Max closed his eyes. But the blow didn't come. He opened them again. The Blackshirt was looking him up and down. He stepped over the rope binding Max to the line of hostages, and Max felt his fingers on his wrists. The Blackshirt wanted his watch. There was a click and Max felt it being slipped off his hand.

The Blackshirt stood in front of him again, holding up the watch. He said something that Max took to mean 'thank you', then he fastened the watch to his own wrist then strode purposefully back to the head of the line. He shouted a single word. Suddenly the Redshirts and the other Blackshirts were grabbing the hostages and forcing them to move.

Max felt sick. That watch was their lifeline – and now the enemy had it.

Sami, Lili and Abby glanced at him desperately. Lukas barely seemed to know where he was. As their forced march continued, he staggered and retched. They had been in the jungle for little more than twenty-four hours, and he was already broken.

They continued to tramp through the rainforest. Panicked thoughts flew through Max's mind. Where were they? In which direction were they headed? How was he going to get the watch back from the tall Blackshirt? Without it, how would they raise the alarm or let the Watchers know their location?

Their abductors seemed to know where they were going. The paths they followed were narrow and hard to navigate, but they were established. Around mid-morning, they started to head uphill. The vegetation thinned out a little, and they finally found themselves on a ridge. From here, they could see for miles over the rainforest. If Max had seen it in a photograph or on TV, he would have been struck by its breathtaking beauty. The forest stretched in all directions to the horizon. Clouds hung over the lower parts. Myriad birds dived and circled. There was no sign of human habitation. Just raw, untouched nature. But this wasn't a picture or a TV show. This was an operation, and the sight only increased Max's sense of panic. The village of Chakunda was nowhere to be seen. The paths they had followed were invisible. A person could wander in this immense forest for months, even years, and never find their way out. As a child, Max had enjoyed the story of Hansel and Gretel, who had left a trail of breadcrumbs in the forest so they could find their way out. They obviously hadn't been lost in the Congo rainforest.

The hostages, with the exception of Lukas, were allowed some water. Then they plunged back downhill and back into the thick, unfriendly vegetation. Max was scratched all over, and he saw that the others were too. Sweat dripped into the cuts on his face, stinging them. Hunger gnawed at his stomach. He started to feel weak and he began to trip more frequently. There was no chance of talking to the others. It took every ounce of concentration just to keep moving through the jungle.

It was early afternoon when they stopped again. They were in a small clearing where a jungle stream fed a deep, still pool. Insects hovered above it. They were so numerous that Max could hear their buzzing from the edge of the clearing. He didn't like the idea of stopping here. It felt like a place where wild animals would come to drink. But the Blackshirts were insistent. He had the impression that there was something they wanted to do here. They forced the hostages to sit in a line. The Redshirts patrolled up and down while the Blackshirts, led by Babaka, spoke in low voices.

'What's happening?' Lili whispered.

'I don't know,' Max said, but he had a bad feeling. He couldn't take his eyes off the Blackshirts, who were pointing back towards the hostages and nodding. He glanced at Sami and Abby, who were also staring across the clearing. Lukas, however, stared, motionless, at the ground, almost as if he was in a daydream. Max thought he saw his hands shaking.

One of the Blackshirts had a bag slung over his shoulder. He opened it and removed a shirt. It was red. Babaka took it and walked over to the hostages. He held it up and spoke. Roland, who was sitting next to Max, whispered a translation. 'He is asking who wants to become a Redshirt.'

Babaka turned to two of his fellow Blackshirts and nodded at them. They stepped forward. At first Max thought they were approaching all the cadets, but they homed in on Abby and Lili. The girls glanced nervously at each other as the Blackshirts untied them and forced them to their feet.

'What's happening?' Sami demanded. 'Hey, what are you doing with them?' At the same time, Max jumped to his feet. Babaka swiped him hard around the face, and Max fell to the ground again. On Babaka's command, the girls were led to the far side of the jungle pool, while Max watched helplessly, his head ringing. The Blackshirts positioned the girls so that they were facing the cadets. They raised their weapons and pointed them at the girls so they couldn't run away. Then Babaka spoke again. He marched along the line of hostages as he talked. Some of the younger ones started to cry. Roland, who seemed to have forgotten about hiding his face, stared at him in horror.

'What's he saying?' Max demanded, not bothering to lower his voice. 'What's going on?'

Roland could barely get the words out. 'He's offering a red shirt to the person who . . .' His voice cracked. 'To the person who will shoot them.'

'*No!*' Max bellowed. He struggled against the ropes tying him to the others. Sami did the same. But they weren't going anywhere. They *couldn't* go anywhere. They were helpless.

Babaka kept on talking and Roland hesitantly translated. 'He says . . . he says they are being punished for attacking his comrades back in the village. He says this is what we must expect if we fight Oscar Juwani's people.'

'Tell him it won't happen again,' Max said. 'If they let Lili and Abby go, they won't hear a peep out of us.'

Roland started to translate, but Babaka shouted over him. 'He's . . . he's saying it again,' Roland said. 'A red shirt for the person who will shoot both girls.'

Desperately, Max scanned the line of hostages. With some relief, he saw that nobody was taking Babaka up on his offer. They avoided his gaze and visibly shrank from him. Then one of the hostages – a boy of perhaps thirteen, who was tied four places along from Roland – stood up. Max felt an icy sensation in his stomach as he realised the boy was volunteering. 'Don't be stupid,' he hissed. 'Sit down. Roland, tell him to sit down.'

Roland mumbled something, but Max couldn't hear what. Babaka appeared delighted. He approached his volunteer with open arms, almost as if he was going to hug him.

'I'll do it.'

At first Max was confused. He thought the volunteer was speaking English and wondered why he hadn't heard him do that before. But then he realised it wasn't the volunteer who had spoken. It was Lukas.

'I'll do it,' Lukas repeated.

Babaka turned. He was no longer interested in the original volunteer, and it was plain that he understood what Lukas had said. He strutted over to him. When he reached Lukas, he bent down and pulled the cadet to

63

his feet. Lukas stood shakily, but he held Babaka's gaze.

'What are you doing, mate?' Max said carefully.

Lukas didn't reply to him. He merely repeated the same words: 'I'll do it.'

Babaka hesitated. Perhaps he was wondering whether this was a trick – a way for Lukas to get himself untied and with a gun in his hand. Max was wondering the same thing. He held his breath as Babaka called one of his comrades over and instructed him to untie Lukas. While this was being done, he raised his submachine gun and pointed it directly at Lukas's head. He didn't speak – but he didn't need to. His meaning was clear: try anything stupid and I'll kill you.

The Blackshirts led Lukas to the edge of the pool. The two girls had narrowed eyes. Like Max, they obviously suspected that Lukas had some kind of plan. But what was it?

Nobody spoke. Even the buzzing of the insects above the pool seemed quieter. Max's muscles were tense. He searched the clearing for points where he could quickly exit into the jungle. But that was impossible while he was still tied to the line of hostages. You'd better have something good, Lukas, he thought.

One of the Blackshirts handed Lukas his assault rifle. Lukas shook his head, handed the weapon back and pointed to something hanging from the Blackshirt's belt. It was a handgun. The Blackshirt looked askance at

Babaka, who shrugged and nodded. The Blackshirt gave Lukas the handgun. Lukas held it expertly. The gang members, with their assault rifles and submachine guns, shifted nervously and retrained their weapons directly on Lukas. Only Babaka seemed unconcerned. He watched almost greedily as Lukas switched off the handgun's safety catch, raised his arm and pointed his weapon at the girls.

But something wasn't right. When he was tied to the other hostages, Lukas's hands had trembled. Now he seemed completely calm. His right arm, which held the gun, was relaxed. He supported the weapon with his left hand like the expert he always was whenever Max had seen him on the gun range back at the training ground of Valley House.

He was preparing to take a shot.

'Ah, c'mon, Lukas,' Abby said. 'You're not thinking of doing anything stupid, are you?'

He didn't reply. He just kept his gun raised and his hands steady.

Abby and Lili stared at him, horror-struck. An expression of horrible realisation crept over their faces. An expression that said: he's going to shoot.

'Lukas!' Max and Sami shouted in unison. '*No!*'

Lukas didn't seem to hear them.

Abby and Lili stared at each other. Something seemed to pass between them. Then they stared back at Lukas.

They closed their eyes and drew deep breaths – so deep that they looked barrel-chested.

Lukas fired two shots in quick succession. The girls crumpled to the ground.

8

Murderer

Max didn't know whether to scream or cry. Truth was, he couldn't do either. He could barely breathe. He just stared, disbelieving.

The gunshots echoed in his ears. Crowds of birds rose up, disturbed by the shots, and the calls and screeches of the jungle animals died away. Lukas lowered his weapon. He turned to Babaka and handed it over. Babaka returned it to its owner then put his arm around Lukas's shoulder. It was a welcoming, brotherly gesture. Lukas glanced at Max but couldn't hold his gaze. One of the gang members gave Lukas the red shirt.

Numb, Max stared across the pond to where Abby and Lil lay, motionless. To his left, Sami was straining against the ropes, desperate to get to the girls, tears streaming down his face. But, like Max, he was held fast. In any case, with their hands tied behind their backs, they were in no position to administer first aid.

'Lukas,' Max whispered, 'CPR . . . stem the bleeding . . .' His voice was so hoarse he could barely hear himself. Two of the younger hostages were crying. Lukas didn't even glance at them. He was too busy putting on his red shirt. Babaka said something to a couple of his Blackshirts. They started to stroll around the pool to the girls, looking relaxed. One of them even laughed. A ferocious anger welled up in Max. If he'd had a weapon to hand, he'd have used it. He wanted to scream at the Blackshirts to leave Abby and Lili alone. He didn't want them anywhere near his friends. What were they going to do? Something awful? Or just dump them in a shallow grave?

They didn't get the chance. They were halfway to the corpses when they suddenly stopped, statue still. Slowly, they started to back away, treading gingerly. At first, Max couldn't see why. Then he saw what was blocking their path.

It was a snake, and it was rising slowly into the air. It must have been long because its head reached the men's waists. It swayed hypnotically. Suddenly it hissed. The two Blackshirts backed away more quickly. Max could see they were terrified. This was plainly a highly venomous snake. Max was so desperately angry he found himself wishing that the snake would strike.

It did.

The Blackshirts were six or seven metres from the snake when its head darted forward and a more aggressive hiss filled the clearing. The Blackshirts jumped back as a spray of liquid jetted from the snake's mouth. Their caution deserted them and they sprinted back to the others, leaving Abby and Lili's bodies where they lay. The snake coiled itself back down to the ground but stayed where it was – like a guardian stopping anyone from approaching the girls.

The snake had scared the gang members and the hostages alike. There was a good deal of shouting. The hostages were forced onto their feet, Max and Sami included. Max's knees buckled as he tried to stand. The horror of what had just happened had overwhelmed him. Two of his closest friends – who was he kidding? Two of his *only* friends – were dead, killed by another friend. It couldn't be real. He felt bile rise to the back of his throat and thought he was going to vomit.

Lukas was not returned to the line of hostages. He was surrounded by other gang members. Despite their hurry to get away from the clearing, some of them slapped his back and shook his hand. He was now trusted by them because he had performed the ultimate act: murder in cold blood. The gang members' glee only served to make Max angrier and more desperate. His friends were dead. *Dead* . . .

A Redshirt with a stick was next to him, threatening to beat him if he didn't start moving. He staggered forward. Sami, apparently as horrified as Max, did the same. The Redshirt shouted at Max to keep moving. He stumbled on.

Max moved as if he was in a trance. The vegetation

was just as thick as before, the air as humid and the insects as voracious. He noticed none of it. Sweating and exhausted, he followed the line of hostages, unable to think of anything but what had just happened. He kept reliving it, hoping that somehow the tape in his mind might change and give him a different ending. But the ending was always the same: the sound of the shots, Abby and Lili collapsing to the ground, and Lukas receiving praise from his new friends.

Then the tears came. Once they had started, they didn't stop. They burned his cheeks. He was gulping for air like a distraught child, his shoulders shaking, his nose streaming. He had seen people die before, but this was different. Abby and Lili were like sisters to him. They were gone, and he felt as if his world had ended.

He didn't know how far they walked or for how long. Sometime in the early afternoon they stopped again for a swig of water and a mouthful of plantain that was growing nearby. Max and Sami found themselves crouching together on the ground, their hands still tied behind their backs. Sami's face was a mess. Tears had smeared the dirt on his cheeks and his eyes were red and sore. Max guessed he looked the same. 'I . . . I don't believe it,' Sami whispered. Like Max, he was having trouble holding it together. 'If I hadn't seen it happen, I *wouldn't* believe it.'

Lukas was sitting with the Blackshirts. He had taken his plastic Ziploc bag of biscuits out and was offering them around. Somehow that simple, friendly gesture sickened Max. 'Me neither,' he said. 'I thought he had been acting weird, but . . .'

'Is he brainwashed?' Sami said. 'That's what happens to people in this cult after all.'

'He must be.'

'Will he try to kill *us*?'

Max had no answer. But thinking of how calm and collected Lukas had been when he took the shots made him shiver. 'I don't know,' he said.

'The mission is over,' Sami said. 'Lukas will eventually tell them who we are and what we are doing. And then . . .' He couldn't finish the sentence.

'And then we go the same way as Abby and Lili,' Max said. The thought had already occurred to him, but it didn't make him scared. His grief was too overpowering.

Sami nodded. 'If you had the watch, you could activate it,' he said.

That was no help. Max didn't have the watch. It was strapped to Babaka's wrist. It was out of play unless he could somehow get it back, and he saw no way of doing that.

'I wish I could speak to Lukas,' Sami said.

'I don't,' Max said. 'He's a murderer. I don't want anything to do with him ever again.'

Sami inclined his head. 'You sound like Roland,' he said.

'What do you mean?'

71

'What was it you told him? That this is what Oscar Juwani does. He takes ordinary young people and forces them to do terrible things. That he changes who they are. That it could happen to any of us.'

'Lukas isn't an ordinary young person,' Max said. 'He's a Special Forces Cadet.'

'Even Special Forces Cadets get it wrong. We're living proof of that, hey?'

Max scowled at his friend. He knew he was behaving badly, but the pain of losing Abby and Lili was too raw. He started to feel angry at his earnest young friend for not sharing his new-found hatred of Lukas. 'Well,' he said, 'if you hadn't insisted on attacking those thugs back in the village, maybe they wouldn't have chosen Abby and Lili as their victims.'

Max instantly felt guilty for what he'd said, but was too angry to apologise.

Sami took a deep breath. 'I think that if we could speak to him,' he said, much more quietly than before, 'we could get him back. The Lukas who did that isn't the real Lukas. He's an imposter . . . Wait, what's that?'

Sami pointed urgently into the vegetation. Max turned quickly. At first he saw nothing but the familiar tangle of broad leaves, tree trunks and vines. 'What are you talking about?' he said. Then he saw it – or thought he saw it – just on the edge of his vision.

Eyes.

In an instant they were gone.

Max felt a surge of insane hope. He had only seen those eyes for the tiniest fraction of a second, but they had looked human. He squinted hard, trying to see through the vegetation, wildly fantasising: could the eyes have belonged to Abby or Lili? He told himself not to be stupid. He had watched Lukas shoot them. He had seen them fall to the ground. Anyway, he wasn't even certain what he had seen. The eyes had disappeared and there was no sign of any movement in the vegetation. He turned back to Sami, but didn't get the chance to speak. One of the gang members was approaching, holding a knife with a gleaming five-inch blade. Max tensed. The gang member held up the knife and said something. The hostages who understood him started to murmur. The gang member approached Roland and cut him away from the ropes that tied him to the others, before cutting the cable ties that bound his wrists behind his back. He moved on to the other hostages, then finally to Max and Sami. He seemed reluctant to cut them free, but he did. Max rubbed his wrists, which were sore and scratched. Roland sidled up to them.

'Why are they untying us?' Max asked.

'So we can move more quickly. He told us not to bother running away because, if we do, we'll get lost in the jungle and die. He's right.' He frowned. 'I am sorry about your friends.'

There was no time to reply. The gang members had started shouting, and they were being forced to march on.

They had no chance to speak. The Redshirts and Blackshirts mingled among them, keeping them quiet and forcing them on if they stumbled. They had only gone a few paces when Max saw, on the ground, the empty Ziploc back that had contained Lukas's biscuits. Quickly he bent down, picked it up and shoved it in his pocket. Maybe he'd find a use for it, but he didn't know what that might be.

Lukas and Babaka stayed at the head of the column, well away from Max and Sami. Soon the path began to slope gently downhill, which made the going a little easier. For that, at least, Max was grateful. He was also grateful to have finished his conversation with Sami, whose understanding nature had made Max feel worse about himself. But he couldn't deny his hatred of Lukas, or his sudden understanding of why Roland despised the Redshirts so much . . .

Movement in the vegetation. Again, for just a fraction of a second, Max caught sight of something. A human shape, camouflaged in the greenery.

Then it was gone.

Or had he imagined it?

He shook his head. His mind was surely playing tricks. It was the stress. The grief. The vegetation was too thick. This part of the forest was deserted. And face it, Max, he told himself, you're not seeing who you think you're seeing. Abby and Lili are dead.

Aren't they?

Nobody else seemed to have noticed anything. The hostages tramped along, their heads down. Many were rubbing their painful wrists. Some sobbed with fear and exhaustion. Even the gang members were more subdued. They seemed nervous. Perhaps it was the sight of the aggressive snake that had done it. Perhaps it was something else. They seemed as tired as the hostages, and just as eager for this journey to be over.

Max wished he had a plan. As soon as they reached their destination, Lukas only had to reveal their identity and surely Juwani's soldiers would kill him and Sami. If only he could find some way to grab his watch from Babaka. Then he could raise the alarm. But that was impossible. They were dominated by the armed gang members, who would kill him without a second thought, he knew that. Anyway, the harder he tried to work out a strategy, the more muddled his mind became. All he could think about was Abby and Lili. His thoughts filled him with such grief that his head wouldn't clear. It was all he could do to put one foot in front of the other.

Someone at the head of the column shouted. Max stopped walking. A couple of Blackshirts were running back. Max caught sight of Lukas, scrambling back with the others amid shouts and panic. He turned to Roland. 'What is it?' he said. 'What are they all so scared of?'

Roland cocked his head, trying to understand the shouts. 'I don't know. I think it's – '

Before he could finish his sentence, an immense roar filled Max's ears. There was no doubt that it was aggressive, and although Max couldn't tell what direction it was coming from, it sounded close.

Roland grabbed his arm. 'It's a gorilla,' he hissed. 'A silverback. Don't move.'

9

Silverback

As soon as Roland said it, Max knew what he had seen in the forest. Not Abby and Lili. Of course not. Those eyes, so human, must have belonged to the gorilla whose roar they had just heard, or one of its troop. It must have been following them for at least an hour.

'I thought gorillas were peaceful animals,' Max muttered.

Roland nodded. 'Normally,' he said. 'But if they feel threatened . . .'

There was another roar. Roland winced. The thugs were suddenly more preoccupied by the danger up ahead than by the hostages. They were talking furiously to each other and many were priming their weapons, getting ready to shoot. But there was still no sign of the beast. The gang members looked to Babaka for guidance. He pointed at two of the Blackshirts and indicated for them to take the lead. They didn't look thrilled at the prospect, but didn't argue. They shifted their rifles onto their shoulders and walked gingerly on.

The rest of the group followed, not in a line this time but in distinct groups, for protection. Lukas was a couple of groups ahead, next to Babaka, so Max couldn't speak to him even if he'd wanted to. Max fell in alongside Sami. 'We need to get the watch,' he whispered to his friend. Sami didn't reply. His expression was intense. 'Mate,' Max said, 'you're not going to do anything stupid, right?' They might have argued, but he couldn't face anything happening to Sami.

Sami didn't seem to hear him. He had upped his pace and was moving towards the front of the group. The thugs didn't pay him any attention. Nor did they notice Max following him. Max didn't know what Sami intended to do, but he was desperate to keep him out of trouble.

The path led to another clearing. This was not a natural clearing. It was roughly circular and as wide as a couple of buses, and the remaining trees were burned. The gang members and their hostages congregated at its edge, Lukas keeping his distance from the other cadets. Several of the thugs had their weapons raised, but there was no sign of any gorilla. The jungle was uncharacteristically quiet.

Until . . .

Another roar split the air. It made the hair on Max's neck stand up. For a second he was more scared for himself than he was distraught by the loss of Abby and Lili. He spun around, trying to see the source of the noise. He wasn't the only one. He couldn't see anything through the thick vegetation, and he had to suppress the urge to run.

'*There!*'

It was Roland who spoke, in English first, then in his own dialect. He was pointing across the clearing. Max couldn't see anything at first, other than a tangle of vegetation. But then there was another chilling roar, and movement, and Max saw a face, then a body.

The gorilla moved forward into the clearing. Max was unprepared for its size. It walked on all fours. Its forearms, immense and hairy, were like tree trunks. Its shoulders were broad and powerful, its head immense. From where he was standing, Max could just see a few wisps of silver on its back, and was struck once more by its strangely human expression.

Then the gorilla roared again, and there was nothing human about that. Its teeth were long and wolf-sharp. It stood on its hind legs and beat its chest. Standing like that, it was taller, broader and stronger than any of the humans facing it. Max wondered if it was protecting its troop. The sheer power of its presence made his legs go weak.

That the gorilla intended to attack was beyond question. The sheer aggression of its behaviour made that clear. And it was clear to the thugs as well as to Max. They weren't as brave as they liked to make out, however. Several shrank back. A couple lowered their weapons and disappeared into the vegetation. Only one, a Blackshirt with unruly wiry hair, had the courage to step forward and aim his weapon directly at the gorilla, ready to shoot.

The gorilla didn't know the danger it was in. It thumped back down onto four feet and thundered towards the humans. Some screamed. Others scattered. Max grabbed one of the younger hostages, who was standing right behind him, and pushed him out of the way towards the trees.

The guy with the gun was shaking, but he managed to keep the rifle trained on the advancing gorilla. His finger was on the outside of the trigger guard. As the gorilla thundered towards him he moved it to the trigger, ready to kill the beast.

'No!' Sami shouted.

'Sami!' Max urged. 'Don't!' But he was too late. Sami had thrown himself at the gunman. A shot rang out, and the retort was so loud and close that Max started violently. But Sami had knocked the Blackshirt sideways. The bullet did not find its target; it flew harmlessly into the trees.

The sound of the bullet had made the gorilla stop. It had also apparently enraged it, because it rose to its hind legs again and roared once more. Then it continued its charge.

'Sami!' Max shouted, for Sami had positioned himself

directly in the path of the animal. 'Get out of the way! It'll kill you!' Lukas stepped forward, alarmed. Everyone else, hostages and thugs alike, whether armed or not, retreated. It was obvious to Max that Sami was putting himself in mortal danger. The gap between him and the gorilla was closing fast.

'Stay back!' Sami hissed. As he spoke, he seemed to shrink. He bowed his head and clasped his arms in front of his chest. He bent forward and bent his knees. Max understood immediately what he was doing: presenting himself to the gorilla as smaller, submissive and less of a threat.

Sami's actions had an immediate effect on the gorilla. It stopped its charge, though it remained on all fours just five paces from him. A deep, rumbling growl escaped its throat. It certainly didn't sound friendly, but it was not as aggressive as before.

Sami's gaze locked with the gorilla's. The gorilla inclined its head. The growling stopped, replaced by heavy breathing.

The gang members and hostages had melted back into the vegetation. Only Max and the Blackshirt who had tried to shoot the gorilla remained in the clearing. The Blackshirt was on the ground, too scared to move. Certainly too scared to raise his rifle. Sami took a careful step forward. The gorilla growled a little louder, then fell quiet. Very slowly, still keeping himself small, Sami approached him.

Max held his breath. He didn't want to speak, in case he distracted the gorilla. He remembered reading in a survival manual that aggressive gorillas could be calmed by submissive behaviour and mutual grooming. It had never been part of their Special Forces Cadets training, however. He wondered how Sami had learned it, growing up in war-torn Syria. He felt his body tingle with tension as Sami reached out and placed his hand on the gorilla's right forearm. He stayed like that for maybe ten seconds. The gorilla trembled but didn't attack. Sami picked a scrap of dry leaf from his fur. Another sound escaped the gorilla's throat, but this time it was more contented than aggressive. It raised its other arm and returned the gesture, gently picking at Sami's hair.

Max didn't dare move. He thought something had passed between Sami and the gorilla. Then there was a sudden movement from the Blackshirt with the gun. He pushed himself up from his prone position and took aim at the gorilla.

'No!' Max shouted, but his voice was drowned out by the gorilla's roar. The animal seemed to know what was happening. Before the thug could take a shot, the gorilla reared up onto its hind legs again and threw itself at the gunman. One massive forearm swiped the Blackshirt's head, throwing him to the ground. The gun went off. Again, the bullet flew harmlessly into the forest. The thug lay on his back, unconscious. He had dropped his weapon and it lay to one side. The gorilla snarled and approached its adversary. Max thought he was going to finish the thug off.

But then Sami was there, between them. He kept himself small but locked gazes with the gorilla. The animal stopped and growled. He reared up again and beat his chest. Then, back down on all fours, he tipped his head to one side. It was a strangely human gesture. Sami imitated it. The gorilla turned and ran back towards the forest, where it disappeared into the vegetation.

Max exhaled in relief. Sami was watching the place where the gorilla had disappeared. He didn't seem to notice that the man on the ground was stirring, or that the other gang members and their hostages were venturing back into the clearing from their hiding places in the vegetation. The gorilla's roars and the retort of the gun had momentarily silenced the jungle, but the noise gradually grew, and with it the thugs' confidence. One of the Blackshirts seized Sami's arm and pulled him to where the other hostages stood. Other gang members started shouting, and in the confusion Max found himself standing next to Lukas.

'Sami needs to stop drawing attention to himself,' Lukas said. 'He'll get himself into trouble. He'll get you into trouble too.'

In the tension of the previous minutes, Max had almost

forgotten his anger and his grief. Now they flooded back. He could barely stand the sight of his former friend. 'Don't talk to me ever again, Redshirt,' he spat.

Suddenly Babaka was there, dragging Lukas away from the hostages. Another thug pulled Max over to Sami.

'That was quite a show,' Max said. 'Where d'you learn to do that?'

'In a book,' Sami replied. 'I never thought I'd ever have to try it out.'

As Sami spoke, Max saw Roland staring at him as if he was a lunatic. Max loyally stared Roland down, even though he agreed with him. 'Could have gone either way,' he said.

'Gorillas are endangered,' Sami said. 'Nobody should be shooting them.'

'You know what else is endangered?' Max said. 'Us. Seriously, Sami, I've already lost two friends today. I don't want to lose another.'

Sami shrugged. 'They're endangered,' he repeated, as if that dealt with all Max's worries. 'We have to do the right thing. It's our only option.' He glanced over at Lukas. 'What did he say?'

'Nothing worth repeating,' Max said. He gave Sami a faint smile. 'A book, huh?'

'What?' Sami said. 'We had books in Syria too, you know. And it's quite boring, waiting for people to drop a bomb on you. Gives you plenty of time to read.'

Despite everything, and although his eyes were crusty with tears, Max couldn't help laughing. Sami was his only friend in the world now. He might be a bit crazy, but Max wouldn't have him any other way.

10

The Stronghold

Max's laugh didn't last long. Soon they were trekking through the jungle again. They moved more slowly this time. The gang members were on edge, thanks to their encounter with the gorilla. They surrounded the hostages like a close protection team, aiming their rifles out into the forest as they picked their way through the vegetation. Max had no idea how they knew which way to go. He guessed they were familiar with the area. He was completely lost.

Anyway, his mind was on other things. With Abby and Lili gone, and Lukas brainwashed by the enemy, their mission was at an end. If he and Sami wanted to survive, they had three options. Escape into the jungle, where they would soon be lost and unlikely to survive more than a couple of days. Or activate the PLB, which was currently fixed around Babaka's wrist. Impossible; they couldn't even get close. So they had to go with the third option: stick with the hostages, keep quiet and hope an opportunity to activate the PLB presented itself.

None did. Max plodded along, sweating and exhausted. The air buzzed with insects and his skin was raw with their bites. From time to time, he thought he saw movement in the vegetation alongside their convoy – a shape that looked vaguely human. But it always disappeared when he tried to pinpoint it. Maybe it was more gorillas. Or maybe it was something else. He was too tired to think about it, or even to be scared.

It was as the light, and the sounds of the jungle, were fading that Max realised the vegetation was thinning out. It was subtle at first: the path was a little wider and the thickets through which they had to force themselves less frequent. Before long, it was obvious. Tree stumps lined the path, and there were frequent man-made clearings, where the vegetation had been cut away. Max caught the distant reek of woodsmoke, just as he had done in the village. The thugs seemed more relaxed. They still brandished their weapons but were no longer pointing them out into the jungle. The Blackshirts even shared some jokes and laughed loudly.

'I think their stronghold is close,' Max whispered to Sami. Sami nodded. No sooner had he done this than the convoy ground to a halt. Babaka shouted something. Max couldn't understand him, but he made out the words 'Oscar Juwani' and felt ice in his stomach. Sami didn't seem to be paying attention. He was searching for something.

'What is it?' Max said.

'Where is Roland?' Sami asked.

There was no sign of him. 'How long has he been gone?' Max said.

'I don't know. I wasn't checking on him. He must have slipped away.'

'He was definitely there when you made friends with the gorilla,' Max said. 'So I guess he must have left in the last couple of hours.'

'Do you think we will see him again?' Sami said.

'I don't know. But put it this way: he knew Oscar Juwani's people were coming to the village and he didn't run away then.'

'You think he wanted to be caught? Like us?'

'Work it out,' Max said. 'Oscar Juwani killed his brother. I think Roland might have something to say about that.'

'He can't fight Oscar Juwani and his thugs by himself,' Sami said.

'No,' Max said, 'he can't. And neither can we.'

'What are we going to do?'

'Nothing,' Max said. He didn't like sounding so negative in front of Sami, but he couldn't hide it. 'It's over, Sami. It was over when Lukas . . .' He couldn't finish the sentence.

'If we could only get our hands on that watch . . .' Sami said.

Max had to bank down his anger. There was no way – *no way* – they could get the watch back. He tried to change the subject. 'Hey, did you notice something – or someone – following us this afternoon?'

Sami nodded.

'You think it was your new best friend?' Max asked. And when Sami didn't respond, he said, 'The gorilla.'

'I don't know,' Sami said. 'I don't think so. I think he would prefer to stay clear of humans.'

'Wise move,' Max said darkly. 'Especially *these* humans.'

The thugs were hurrying them on again. They didn't seem to have noticed that Roland was missing. They seemed too keen to reach their destination to count their prisoners. The convoy upped its pace. The trees grew thinner, the smell of woodsmoke stronger. Then there was another smell. Fetid and unpleasant. It was human sewage – and it was getting stronger.

Then they were on the edge of a clearing, perhaps the size of a couple of football pitches. All the trees had been cut down. Some still lay where they fell, while others had been moved to the edge of the clearing. Patches of vegetation had been burned away, leaving black areas. Some were still smoking. The jungle itself had been scary but beautiful. This was ugly – as if the forest had been cut and wounded, and this was an enormous scar.

To the right, at one end of the clearing, there was a small but fast-moving stream. Fires were dotted around the clearing. Some of them were being used for cooking, with spits erected in front of them and meat roasting. It smelled rancid and gamey. Max had a nasty feeling it was monkey. There were a few rough shelters and lean-tos made from branches and other jungle foliage. They were not well built, but tumbledown and surrounded by debris. Deep pits yawned around the edge of the clearing. Some emitted a dirty yellow smoke.

It was hard to be sure how many people were there. Max guessed about a hundred and fifty. Without exception they wore black, red or blue tops.

At the far side of the clearing was a raised plateau, about house height. It backed onto thick, impenetrable jungle. The plateau must have formed naturally; to construct it by hand would have taken years. A rough staircase, hewn out of rock and guarded by two Blackshirts, led up to the plateau. On top there was a hut, larger and more soundly built than any of the shelters down below. Several Blackshirts stood guard around it.

'I reckon that's Oscar Juwani's place,' Max whispered to Sami, who stood next to him. Sami nodded.

Next to the plateau stood a tall, sturdy tree. A large bamboo cage dangled from a thick branch, fifteen metres from the ground. The other end of the rope was tied to the base of the tree. From this distance Max couldn't be sure, but it looked as if the cage contained people. Three, maybe four, insanely cramped. He suspected that this was the SAS team the cadets had been brought in to rescue. The team had no way of escaping from their suspended prison, and Max didn't want to think about what the conditions were like in there. Were they starving? Were they ever let down to use the toilet? Were they even still alive?

There were a number of other bamboo cages, nine or ten perhaps, but these were on the ground. They were larger than the suspended cage, and empty, but Max reckoned he had a pretty good idea of where he and Sami would be spending the night.

He examined the people in the clearing. None of them looked older than sixteen or seventeen, and many looked much younger than that. Most were boys, but there were girls too: two thirds to one third, Max estimated. Only the Blackshirts were armed. Max could only see three Blackshirts – all were male, and they had a swagger to them. It was clear, even from a distance, that they liked being in charge. They were waving their arms about and giving instructions to the Redshirts. The Redshirts moved slowly around the clearing, working. Some stoked the fires, others carried boxes, a few were cooking – but their jobs were not obviously unpleasant. Those jobs fell to the Blueshirts, who were digging pits around the edge of the clearing, or filling them in with soil. Some of these pits were obviously latrines – Max saw a Redshirt urinating into one. But surely they weren't all latrines?

Max didn't want to dwell on what other purpose they might serve. Some Blueshirts were chopping logs – a large log pile lay under a wooden frame with a palm-leaf roof. Some washed clothes in old metal baths.

But one boy in particular drew Max's attention. He was not far from the raised plateau. Two Redshirts had just knocked him to the ground. One sat on the back of the Blueshirt's legs, pinning him down. The other had a thin length of rope which he was using to whip the Blueshirt's back. The boy's howls could be heard all around the clearing. Some of the Blackshirts pointed and laughed. A few Redshirts dared to look. Without exception, the other Blueshirts averted their gaze, obviously scared that if they paid too much attention, they could meet the same fate. Sami, who stood next to Max, tensed.

'Not now, Sami,' Max whispered. 'It's not the time.'

Sami nodded almost imperceptibly, but he didn't stop watching.

Babaka shouted something and Max felt himself being poked in the back. It was one of the Blackshirts, urging him on with the barrel of his rifle. Max stumbled forward, down a shallow slope. Their arrival caused a few of the Blackshirts in the clearing to call out and jog towards them. They greeted the cadets' Blackshirt guards like brothers, hugging them and slapping each other on the back. There was a flurry of conversation. Babaka was explaining to the others what had happened on their journey. Max couldn't understand his words, of course. But he knew what Babaka was saying when he pointed at Lukas and mimed taking two shots with obvious approval. Max's anger and grief returned tenfold. Lukas, who was standing well apart from the others, remained stony-faced, staring into the middle distance. It was as if Babaka's story had no effect on him. The new Blackshirts treated him with a certain respect. Then Babaka pointed at Sami and appeared to be explaining what had happened with the gorilla. Max found himself staring at the watch on his wrist. Babaka sneered at Max. He pointed at the watch then at himself, as if to say, *It's mine.*

Then the Blackshirt the gorilla had hit took up the story. His face was badly bruised. His mates eyed Sami as if he was a troublemaker. Max, standing next to him, felt the heat of their glare too. He knew they should expect rough treatment. And soon. The gang members were splitting up the hostages. Max, Sami and most of the others were dragged towards the pits on the edge of the clearing. Lukas was being ushered in a different direction: towards the heavily guarded plateau. Max wondered if he had noticed Roland's disappearance. If he had, would he tell the Blackshirts? Or would he tell Oscar Juwani? Because that was surely where they were taking him.

Lukas glanced back as he was led away. For the first time since he had shot Abby and Lili, Max saw a new expression in his face. He looked haunted, uncertain and scared.

Max didn't care how Lukas felt. They were no longer friends and Max had his own problems to deal with.

11

The Pit

The red shirt they had given Lukas to wear over his other shirt stank of sweat – and of something else too. There were dark stains on the cuffs. Blood, he assumed. He didn't want to know who had worn the shirt last, and he didn't want to wear it now. He was not one of them. He had to try hard not to stumble as Babaka led him across the clearing. The trek through the jungle had exhausted him. His legs were weak and his mind numb with fatigue. Part of him was hungry, but he doubted he could eat anything. The foul reek that hung around this place was enough to make anybody lose their appetite. Worse than that, though, was the look Max and Sami had given him. His friends hated him.

He understood. In their shoes, he'd feel the same.

Everyone stared at him as he passed. Here, in the centre of the clearing, they were mostly Redshirts, like Lukas. Their eyes were dead. He remembered what Angel had said during their briefing. *The things these kids are forced to do . . . you wouldn't want to know about it.*

What had they done? he wondered. Who had they killed? Had they shot their best friends, like Lukas had? Whatever it was, he could tell that their actions haunted them. They had done things that made returning to their previous lives impossible. They were criminals. Killers. It meant they were locked in to Oscar Juwani's cult for life.

He heard a shriek. The boy with the blue shirt was still being beaten. Lukas turned away, unable to watch. He walked past a roaring fire, over which several monkeys were being roasted on a spit. The smell turned his stomach. He stared in the direction Babaka was leading him: towards the rough staircase leading up to the plateau.

There were two guards at the bottom of the staircase: aged about fifteen, in black shirts and torn trousers and carrying AK-47s. They obviously recognised Babaka and stepped aside to let him pass, but when Lukas tried to follow they blocked his path. One of them forced him to raise his arms. The other patted him down, searching for concealed weapons. Lukas was unarmed, of course, so the guard found nothing. As he was patting down Lukas's chest, however, his hand stopped at the hard circle of his Special Forces Cadets challenge coin, sewn into his first shirt. But it wasn't weapon-shaped. Perhaps the guard thought it was just a button. He finished patting Lukas down without comment, then nodded at Babaka and let him pass.

Lukas followed Babaka up the stairs onto the plateau.

From here, he had an excellent view of the whole clearing. He picked out Max and Sami, who were being led to the pits at the far side. Lukas was on a level with the hanging bamboo prison and could see its occupants: four men in military camouflage gear. Their faces were almost black with dirt. They were gaunt and bruised. There was no room for them to lie down, so they sat, their heads lolling listlessly. The caged buzzed with insects, no doubt attracted by the waste and the smell. Lukas *thought* the men were alive, but he couldn't be sure. He shuddered and turned away.

Babaka beckoned to him. Out in the jungle he had been almost friendly, but now he had changed. Lukas thought he seemed nervous as he led his new Redshirt around the large hut on the plateau. Beyond it another fire burned, bigger than the ones in the clearing. There was something more appetising being roasted here. A deer, maybe? Lukas couldn't be sure. He counted five more Blackshirt guards, all armed, two of whom flanked the entrance to the hut. Babaka approached and murmured something to one of the guards. The guard seemed uncertain as he glanced at Lukas, but he shrugged and knocked on the door of the hut. He opened it and disappeared inside. Lukas realised he was holding his breath. Then the guard reappeared and beckoned them in.

Babaka went first. Lukas felt all the Blackshirts watching him. He tried not to show how nervous he felt. Drawing himself up to his full height, he entered the hut.

There were candles burning inside, but it was still dim and it took a few seconds for Lukas's eyes to adjust. Gradually he became aware of his surroundings. The hut was circular, and a lot more comfortable than the rough shacks down in the clearing. There were rugs on the floor and large cushions scattered around. For all the comfort, however, it smelled musty and unclean. Weapons racks adorned the walls, filled with assault rifles, handguns, ammunitions and even a rocket-propelled grenade launcher. Against the far wall was a comfortable armchair. And sitting in the armchair was the most enormous man Lukas had ever seen. Rolls of fat surrounded his jowly face. His vast stomach overhung the armchair. His face was covered with scars and beads of sweat. One of his eyes was milky. He was smoking. Each time he inhaled, his face glowed red. He wore military camouflage gear. In another situation it would have been funny, because he was so ill-suited for physical activity. But nothing about him made Lukas want to laugh. Behind him, hanging on the wall, was a picture of the fat man in his youth, carrying a rifle in each hand. And the man himself oozed danger. His expression was cold. As Babaka spoke to him, he stared directly at Lukas. Then he raised one hand and made a 'shoo' gesture. Babaka turned to leave. Lukas made to follow him.

'Not you,' said the man. His voice was low and harsh. Lukas stopped. He was surprised that the man had spoken in English. Babaka left the hut. The man extinguished his cigarette in a brimming ashtray on a table next to him.

'English?' he said.

'American,' Lukas replied.

'Excellent. I am glad to have the chance to practise your language. The last English-speakers to arrive here –' he looked over one shoulder, as if he could see through the wall of the hut towards the cage hanging from the tree – 'they did not want to chat. And I fear they will not live much longer. We will photograph their bodies when they are dead and show them to the world, so that people will understand what happens if they give Oscar Juwani trouble. What is your name?'

'Lukas.'

'Do you know who I am?'

Lukas did, of course, but he couldn't admit it. It would blow their cover story. 'No,' he said.

The man smiled, as if he knew Lukas was lying. 'My name is Oscar Juwani. And you belong to me. Everybody here belongs to me. Babaka tells me you shot your two friends.'

Lukas stared straight ahead.

'How did it feel, Lukas? How did it feel when you shot them dead? Did you enjoy it?'

Lukas set his jaw. 'A bit,' he said.

'It becomes better, the more you do it,' Oscar Juwani

said. 'You learn to enjoy the way they beg for mercy, and the way they squeal. You will have the chance to do it again. I will find opportunities for you. Maybe you will do it enough to earn one of my black shirts. Would you like that?'

Lukas hesitated. Then he nodded.

Oscar Juwani seemed delighted by this. 'Good.' He chuckled. 'Good. Babaka thinks I should kill you.' The smile dropped from his face and he was suddenly deadly serious again. 'He thinks I should kill you and your friends. He says there is something strange about you all. Something he doesn't trust. Babaka has very good instincts, Lukas. He was going to kill you in the jungle, but you surprised him by shooting the two girls. He was not so sure of himself then, and he knew that if he killed good people I would be angry with him. Would you like to know what happens to people I am angry with?'

Lukas's stomach felt hollow. He nodded.

'Good. Follow me.'

Oscar Juwani stood up with great difficulty. He was sweating and wheezing by the time he was on his feet. Once he was standing, however, he was more agile. He left the hut. Lukas glanced at the weapons on the wall. Part of him wanted to grab one, but he knew that would be the wrong move. There were at least ten armed guards out there. If he presented any kind of a threat, he'd be dead in seconds. So he followed Oscar Juwani outside.

It had grown dark. Darkness fell quickly in the jungle, Lukas had noticed. The fire had been stoked and was blazing fiercely. Oscar Juwani walked round it, flanked by two Blackshirts. Lukas could only see their flickering silhouettes. They had their backs to him and were staring down at something. Lukas moved round the fire and joined them. Oscar Juwani and his two guards stood in front of a sheet of wood, about two metres long and a metre wide. It was weathered but sturdy. Oscar Juwani was wheezing again. Lukas had the feeling that this was out of excitement. He said something to the two Blackshirts. They exchanged a nervous glance and received a sharp word from their boss. That was enough. They moved to either end of the sheet, bent down and shifted it to reveal a hole in the ground.

The hole had been neatly dug: a precise rectangle with straight edges, like a grave. A truly terrible smell wafted out of it, so putrid it made Lukas want to be sick. And there was a sound too. A slithering, hissing, angry sound. Whatever was in that pit had been disturbed by the light, and didn't like it.

'Go ahead, Lukas,' Oscar Juwani said. 'See what's inside.'

Lukas stepped carefully towards the edge of the pit. It was deeper than an adult was tall. At first he couldn't see what was at the bottom, so he squinted. The floor of the stinking pit was moving. He shuddered. He knew what was down there, even before his eyes sorted it all out.

Snakes.

How many? He couldn't tell. Thirty? Forty? Perhaps even more. They were entwined, sinuously moving, all hissing at different frequencies to create a sinister cacophony that made Lukas's hair stand on end. He wanted to turn away, but he couldn't help staring into the pit. He wasn't sure, but he thought he saw the bones of a human hand sticking out, before being hidden by the snakes.

'Black mambas,' Oscar Juwani said. 'One snake holds enough venom to kill forty men.' He gave another curt instruction. The two Blackshirts covered the pit again. Lukas stayed where he was. He could sense Oscar Juwani approach him from behind. He could smell him – sweat and cigarettes – and feel his hot breath next to his ear. 'Maybe,' Oscar Juwani whispered, 'you could be my head Blackshirt. One day. Maybe I will let you kill Babaka. But if I find out that you are not who you say you are, I will let one of the Blueshirts push you into the pit. It will be an excellent rite of passage for them, and you will make a fine meal for my little babies. Do you understand?'

Lukas took a deep breath. He turned. 'I understand,' he said. 'Totally.'

Oscar Juwani clapped his hands. 'Excellent! You must be hungry!' He gave an order, and a couple of Blackshirts removed the roasting animal from its spit. 'Tonight we eat,' Oscar Juwani said. 'Tomorrow we work. Come.'

He took Lukas by the arm and ushered him towards the animal. On the other side of the fire, however, Lukas couldn't help noticing Babaka staring at him with a dark, aggressive expression. He obviously did not like the way Oscar Juwani was putting his arm around Lukas's shoulder, inviting him to eat and treating him like his new favourite.

12

Caged

The edge of the clearing, where the Blackshirts led Max and Sami, was foul. A pall of acrid smoke hung over the area. It came from a couple of pits where rubbish was being burned, and the smell stuck in the back of Max's throat. There was an old metal container full of water with a cup chained to it. It was obviously for drinking, but insects floated on the surface and the water smelled sulphuric. Nobody went near it.

Next to the container was the huge log pile Max had noticed earlier. Nobody was chopping logs any more, however, and the axes had gone. Two Redshirts had filled a basket with logs and were taking them back to one of the cooking fires in the clearing.

There were about thirty Blueshirts here. They made a sorry sight. Most were younger than Max and Sami, but their hands and bare feet were weathered and leathery. Many of them had sores on their legs, and their skin was covered in insect bites. Their shoulders were slumped, their faces slack. They had the bodies of children, but the demeanour of elderly people. Each had a shovel, and they hacked listlessly into the hard ground. They were digging five pits. Max didn't know what for.

A Blackshirt gave Max and Sami a dirty, ill-fitting blue T-shirt each. Max and Sami pulled the garments over their existing clothes. Then the Blackshirt gave them a shovel and pointed to the smallest of the five pits. There were four young Blueshirts there, three boys and a girl. Their shovels hardly made any impression on the ground. When Max and Sami joined them, they barely seemed to notice the new arrivals. They just stared at the ground and went through the motions of digging. One of them, a boy of about eleven, was crying. It didn't take long to see why. His hands were bleeding. The wooden handle of his shovel was stained, and blood dripped down his fingers. Max wondered how long he had been digging. Hours? Days? However long it was, he needed medical care.

The Blackshirts were walking away. There was clearly no need to guard these children closely. They were too exhausted to run. In any case, where would they go? Into the jungle where their wounds would become infected and one dark night would see them off? No. They were stuck, just as surely as if they were chained. Max sidled up to the boy. He gave him a reassuring smile then gestured for the boy to show Max his hands. At first the boy didn't want to, but Max gently insisted. The boy held out his palms. They were red-raw and glistening, with streaks of pus along one side of his right hand. Max knew that if the infection got worse – which it would, in this humidity – it could enter the boy's bloodstream. If that happened, the boy could die within hours. He needed medical attention, but there was none available. Max would have to improvise.

None of the Blackshirts was paying any attention to them. Max lifted the blue T-shirt he had just been given to reveal the khaki shirt he had been wearing since they parachuted in. It was torn in places from their trek through the jungle. That made it easy to rip. Carefully, he tore a couple of long strips from the shirt. He wished they were cleaner, but they would do as temporary bandages to stop any more dirt getting into the boy's wounds. Max gave him an encouraging smile and wrapped the makeshift bandages round his wounded palms. The boy winced but bravely let Max finish. By the time he had finished the second hand, blood was already soaking through the first. The bandages were ragged and insufficient. Max shook his head. They might give the boy a few hours of protection, but if he didn't get proper care soon, his wounds would kill him. He wondered how many Blueshirts had died this way. Many, he was sure of it. He found himself wondering what happened to their bodies. Then it dawned on him why they were digging holes in the ground. No wonder, he thought, that these young people would do anything to win themselves a red shirt. Their survival depended on it. It was that – or dig themselves into an early grave.

The other Blueshirts seemed too scared to watch what was going on. Sami, however, was staring at Max with an oddly approving look. Max realised that he had lost hope when Lukas shot Abby and Lili. Their mission had seemed pointless. Doomed to failure. Sami, however, had not succumbed to that hopelessness. He had believed, despite everything, in the power of doing the right thing.

As usual, Sami had been right.

'We have to do something about this,' Max said. 'It's about more than rescuing the SAS men now. It's about stopping Oscar Juwani. He can't be allowed to continue.'

Sami nodded. 'I agree,' he said. He was a mild young man, but there was something inspiring about his determination. 'The Blackshirts are armed all the time,' he said. 'I think that they *like* killing. The Redshirts have been forced to do it. If we disable the Blackshirts, I think the Redshirts will come quietly. How many Blackshirts do you think there are?'

'I've been counting,' Max said. 'I make it fifteen. But they're heavily armed. We can't risk fighting them without backup. We have to get that watch back somehow.'

They looked up to the plateau where Babaka had led

Lukas. A fire was burning brightly up there, and they could just make out some people standing near it. Max thought one of them might be Lukas, but he was too far away to tell.

'Are you thinking what I'm thinking?' Sami said.

'I don't know. What are you thinking?'

'Lukas is the one who can get closest to Babaka. If we can somehow get him to –'

'No. Lukas is a traitor.'

'Maybe he's just like all the other Redshirts,' Sami said quietly.

'It's different,' Max said. 'He was one of us. I agree we need to get the watch, but I'm not involving him. We can't trust him. If and when we get out of here, I never want to see him again.'

Sami was about to argue, but he didn't get the chance. Night was falling and three Blackshirts approached. The children around them let their shovels fall to the ground, so Max and Sami did the same. The Blackshirts didn't need to issue any instructions. They simply led the Blueshirts – Max and Sami included – towards one of the bamboo cages. It was large enough to take them all, though not comfortably. As they filed in at gunpoint, Max and Sami lingered at the back of the line. The door to the cage didn't look very secure. Maybe, Max thought, they could force it open somehow during the night. If they were last into the cage, they could sit by the entrance and break out.

No chance. Once they were inside the cage, one of the Blackshirts wrapped a long chain several times round the door and locked it with a heavy padlock. He put the key on a string round his neck. Maybe he suspected that Max and Sami had thought about escape, because he leered at them as he did this. Then he and the other Blackshirts turned their backs on the cage and walked through the gloom towards one of the fires burning in the clearing, where the monkeys were being roasted.

The rest of the Blueshirts were too exhausted to do anything but lie on the rough ground. A couple of them tried to talk to Max and Sami, but they had no language in common so they soon gave up and fell asleep. All except one. The boy whose hands Max had tended shuffled up to him. He was shivering and obviously ill. The boy rested his head on Max's knee and began to weep softly. All Max could do to comfort him was to stroke his hair gently – and turn his thoughts to plans of escape.

Night had fallen. The fire outside Oscar Juwani's hut had burned down to glowing coals. What remained of the animal carcass after they had stripped the meat from it was smouldering on the fire. Oscar Juwani had returned to his hut, which was still heavily guarded by Blackshirts. Two remained by the hut's entrance and two more at the top of the steps that led down into the clearing. Several others circled the plateau. They all had assault rifles. Babaka sat on a log by the fire, smoking hand-rolled cigarettes, watching Lukas.

Lukas had been given his own watch point: a tree stump next to the snake pit. His job, Oscar Juwani had explained, one fat hand gripping Lukas's shoulder, was to keep watch on the jungle behind the plateau. It was as thick and impenetrable as any vegetation Lukas had seen in the past forty-eight hours.

Lukas wasn't stupid. He knew this was an unimportant position. Nobody really expected a threat to come from that area, and Lukas had certainly not been trusted with a firearm. He was not there to keep watch. He was there to *be* watched. Oscar Juwani *wanted* to trust him – a sharp-shooting American kid would be a great prize for the leader of this gruesome cult – but he didn't trust him yet. Lukas had been placed close to the snake pit to remind him what would happen if he let Oscar Juwani down. He had got used to the smell and tried not to think about the snakes, but he couldn't help hearing them under the lid as they hissed and seethed from time to time.

The moon was bright. So bright that it cast shadows. Lukas sat with his back to the fire and the hut, but he could see the patrolling Blackshirts by the shadows they cast as they circled the fire. And he could almost feel Babaka's gaze drilling into his back. He was bone tired, but sleep wasn't an option. Sounds drifted up to the plateau from the clearing. Bouts of brutish laughter. Sometimes an aggressive shout. Occasionally a scream. In his mind, a tumult of images. The snakes. Oscar Juwani. Babaka. Sami and the gorilla. And of course, Lili and Abby, and the expressions on their faces in the seconds before he squeezed the trigger.

He stared at his hand. It was shaking. There was no way he could accurately fire a gun, even if he had one.

Time passed. He wanted to walk to the edge of the plateau and see if he could find out what had happened to Max and Sami, but that was impossible. He had to pretend not to care about them. Only then would the Blackshirts start to trust him.

Only then could he get close to Babaka.

Finally, Babaka seemed to have lost interest in him. He had his weapon on his knee. He removed the magazine and held it up, checking it in the moonlight. A wild thought crossed Lukas's mind: he could sprint over to him, grab the watch and activate the PLB. He almost did it. But then, squinting through the moonlight, he realised that the watch wasn't on Babaka's wrist. Good thing too – they'd have killed him, and the others, instantly if he'd acted on his instinct. But he couldn't help wondering where the watch was. In Babaka's pocket, maybe? Somewhere else? Then Babaka caught him staring. He replaced the magazine in the assault rifle then pointed towards the jungle as if to say, *You're supposed to be facing that way.*

Which Lukas did. The moon illuminated the line where the plateau met the jungle. It was a thick knot of scrub, trees, vines and bamboo. And there was nothing to see.

Nothing to see.

Nothing to see.

Then there was a movement.

Lukas blinked. He glanced back at Babaka, but the Blackshirt wasn't there. He had wandered over to the hut and was talking quietly to the guards at the entrance. Lukas squinted back at the jungle, at the place where he had seen movement. At first he saw nothing. Maybe he had imagined it. But then he saw it again. Two broad leaves, head-height from the ground, parted like curtains. And between them was a face.

Lukas's pulse raced. The moon was bright but it wasn't daylight, and the face was a good twenty metres away. He squinted to make out its features.

Suddenly he had the most curious sensation: tension draining from his body like water from a bath.

Lukas inclined his head. He didn't dare speak.

The head nodded. The curtains closed. The face was gone.

Lukas swallowed hard and glanced back over his shoulder. Babaka had finished talking to the two guards and was walking over to the steps. He gave no indication that he'd seen anything, but he looked over suspiciously at Lukas then pointed towards the jungle again before disappearing down the steps.

Lukas turned back and continued his watch, the ghost of a smile on his lips.

13

Ziploc

Max knew he should sleep. He had no chance of getting out of the cage tonight. If he was going to find his watch the following day, he needed his strength.

But sleep was impossible. First there was the lack of comfort: the ground was hard and bumpy. Then there was the steady weeping of the kid with the septic hands. And the moon, bright enough to cast a shadow. And the noise. The Blackshirts were rowdy, at least at first. When they grew quieter, the strange noises of the jungle rang in the air. Max wondered if he would ever get used to them.

He sat there, hugging his knees. Anybody watching him would think that he was just staring into space. He wasn't. The moonlight went to the far edges of the clearing and he could hear Hector in his head, holding forth on one of his favourite themes. *Situational awareness is everything. Whenever you're in an unfamiliar environment, you need to familiarise yourself with your surroundings. Where are your entry and exit points? Where are the danger zones? Where are threats most likely to come from? Where can you take cover? The main difference between a professional soldier and the man in the street is nothing to do with weapons or military gear. It's to do with observation. The more you see, the more you know. And in a theatre of war, knowledge is power.*

Max knew he needed all the power he could get. So he plotted the clearing in his head. The position of the plateau and the tree with the hanging cage. The location of each hut. The opening into the jungle through which they had entered the clearing, and the number of armed guards standing there: three. He estimated how long it would take him to run to the plateau, or from the plateau to the entrance. The thought even crossed his mind that if he really – *really* – needed somewhere to hide, the toilet pit was the place to do it, because who would want to search for him in there?

Next to him, Sami was doing the same. Max could sense him clocking the locations and pinning them in his mind. Stuck in the locked cage, it was all they could do.

'It's going to be a long night,' Sami said after a while. The other Blueshirts seemed to be asleep, even the kid with the damaged hands.

'We've had long nights before, I guess,' Max said. He thought of the care home where he'd been brought up, and of the many nights he had spent wide awake, staring at the same moon that floated above them now. Would he swap places with the old Max? he wondered. The answer came quickly. No. Despite everything, no.

'When I was in Syria,' Sami whispered, 'during the war, the quiet nights were the worst. When they were bombing us, at least we knew what was happening and where bombs were falling. You could try to do something about it. When it was quiet . . .' His voice trailed off. 'Sometimes waiting for a thing to happen is worse than the thing happening,' he said finally. A pause. 'You know Lukas had no choice, don't you?'

'I don't want to talk about –' Max cut himself short. 'What was that?'

'What?'

Max didn't answer. He had seen something on the edge of the clearing. A person, running past Oscar Juwani's stronghold before disappearing into the jungle. 'It looked like . . .'

'Like what?'

Max didn't reply immediately, because he knew how crazy he would sound. 'Nothing,' he whispered. 'I just . . . I thought I saw someone. It's nothing.'

'We should get some sleep,' Sami said.

Max squinted across the clearing again. There was no sign of the figure. 'I wish I could,' he said. 'Do you think the SAS men are alive?'

'Yes,' Sami replied. 'If they were dead, Juwani's men would have burned or buried them. Rotting bodies would attract wild animals, cause disease. There's a reason the Blueshirts are digging those pits, you know. They have to do something with dead bodies. Hey, look!'

Sami pointed towards the plateau. They could just see, through a jumble of huts, the steps leading up to it. A figure was walking down the steps. Max could only make out the figure's silhouette in the darkness, but he recognised the swagger. It was Babaka. At the bottom of the steps he turned and started walking towards Max and Sami. His face was bathed in moonlight. There was no doubt who it was.

'Is he coming here?' Sami asked.

'Yeah,' Max said. 'Quick, pretend to be asleep.'

They lay down, but Max only half closed his eyes so he could watch Babaka approach the cage. He stood just on the other side of the bamboo railings and stared down at them. Max checked out the man's wrist. The watch wasn't there. Babaka stood watching them for about a minute, his face unreadable. Then he turned away and walked back towards the huts. He stopped at one hut, kicked the door open and entered.

'Did you see –' Max started to say.

'No watch,' Sami confirmed.

Silently, they surveyed the hut for five minutes, then ten, waiting to see if Babaka would leave. He didn't. It looked as if he would spend the night there. That was surely his hut.

'Do you think that's where he's left the watch?' Sami said finally.

'Yeah,' Max replied. 'Perhaps. Tomorrow we have to get in there.'

'If they catch us doing that, we'll end up in one of the holes we're digging.'

'I've got a feeling,' Max said, 'that we're going to end up in one of those holes anyway. I'd say we've got nothing to lose, wouldn't you?'

Sami didn't answer. Max went back to plotting the layout of the clearing in his head.

The jungle creatures knew dawn was coming before it grew light. Their cacophony woke Max up. He couldn't remember falling asleep. It must have been in the small hours. His body ached from lying on the hard ground and he felt more tired than he had before he went to sleep.

He immediately sensed that Sami was awake next to him.

'We need a distraction,' Sami said.

Max stretched. 'What?'

'If we're going to get into Babaka's hut, we need a distraction. Something that will get all the Blackshirts looking the other way. The Redshirts too. That will give one of us the chance to slip over to the hut and search it.'

'Agreed,' Max said.

'Maybe one of us can pretend to be ill,' Sami said.

Max shook his head. 'You think they'd care about that?' He pointed at the kid with the sore hands to prove his point. 'The only way we're going to distract the Blackshirts is if they're worried about themselves.'

'How do we do that?'

It was suddenly much lighter. There was movement in the clearing. Figures were stoking the fires with fresh logs.

'Fire,' Max said.

'What?'

'They need fire. They need it to cook, to boil water, to keep animals at bay. And to make fire, they need logs.' He indicated the log pile by the pits they'd been digging. 'Those logs.'

'I don't understand,' Sami said.

'If we set fire to those logs,' Max said, 'I reckon they'll freak out.' He pointed across the clearing towards the stream. 'They made a mistake, I reckon, putting the log pile at the opposite end to the stream. I suppose they were worried about the wood getting wet if the stream flooded. If we set fire to it, it'll keep them all busy ferrying water across the camp to put it out.'

'Maybe,' Sami said uncertainly. 'But how are we going to do that? We don't have matches or anything.' He frowned. 'We could maybe take a burning branch from one of the other fires . . .'

'We don't need to,' Max said. 'We've got everything we need.' Surreptitiously, he put his hand in his pocket and pulled out a corner of the Ziploc bag Lukas had kept his biscuits in.

Sami blinked at him. When he spoke, it was slowly, as if he was explaining something to a small child. 'That is a plastic bag, Max,' he said.

'Glad to see your powers of observation haven't deserted you.'

'You can't make fire with a plastic bag.'

Max winked at him then shoved the corner of the bag back into his pocket. A Blackshirt was marching up to them. Max recognised him as the guy with the key round his neck. He unlocked the padlock and removed the chain from the cage. He barked at the Blueshirts. Some were still asleep, but they woke quickly. They obviously knew better than to linger. They were on their feet in seconds, queuing up to be let out of the cage. Only the little kid with the sore hands moved slowly. He was shivering badly and was having trouble standing. Max pulled him to his feet and, despite an unpleasant glare from the Blackshirt, helped him out of the cage and back towards the pits.

They were allowed a few mouthfuls of water from a plastic canteen, and a tiny portion of stale bread which Max hungrily devoured. After that, the Blueshirts automatically went back to digging. A couple of Blackshirts approached with axes. They held them up. None of the Blueshirts seemed keen on taking one. It was obviously harder work than digging. One of the Blackshirts handed an axe to the kid with the sore hands. Max stepped up to him, pointed out the kid's bandages, and gave the Blackshirt a 'c'mon, be serious' look. He took the axe and pointed to himself. The Blackshirt shrugged. Sami approached the other Blackshirt, took the second axe and he and Max walked over to the logs. There were two piles: the logs that were already split and stacked under the frame, and a larger pile that needed chopping.

'What now?' Sami hissed.

'We chop,' Max said. 'We can't do anything else until the sun is high.' He bent over one of the tree trunks. The bark was dry and papery, with thick patches of dried moss and lichen. He picked some of it off. 'We need this,' he said. 'It'll make good tinder. Then we need smaller fragments of wood to get the fire going.'

'Max,' Sami said, 'you still haven't told me how you're planning to get the fire going.'

'You ever do that magnifying glass thing?' Max said. 'You know, when you concentrate the sun's rays and aim it at an ant or something?'

Sami appeared genuinely puzzled. 'But that would kill the ant,' he said.

'Exactly.'

'I would never kill an ant, Max.'

Max had to smile. 'Right,' he said. 'Anyway, the thing is, you can start a fire with a magnifying glass – or any kind of lens.'

'But we don't have one.'

'Yes, we do,' Max said. 'If you fill a clear plastic bag with water and seal it, it can act like a lens and focus the sun's rays.'

'Are you sure?'

'Well, I've never done it, but I . . .'

'Read about it in a book?'

'Right,' Max said. 'Come on, that Blackshirt is watching us. Let's get chopping. And remember, collect as many splinters of wood as possible so we have some decent kindling.'

They soon realised why none of the other Blueshirts wanted to be on chopping duty. It was hard, hot, back-breaking work. The axes were blunt. Soon the boys were sweating and aching, their hands blistered and their lungs burning. Shards of wood flew up into their faces. As he chopped, Max kept one eye on the kid with the sore hands. He was on his feet but not really digging. He just seemed to be propping himself up on the shovel, obviously too scared to lie down. Max thought he might collapse at any minute, but he couldn't go to his aid. He had to keep a low profile while the sun rose.

When the sun was high enough for its light to start flooding into the clearing, Max estimated it was about 10 a.m. Another half an hour passed before the sun's rays reached the log pile.

'Keep chopping,' Max told Sami. He put down his own

axe, then wandered over to the metal container filled with stale water. He held his breath so he didn't have to inhale its rank smell. A nearby Blackshirt glanced over at him, but turned away when he saw Max splash the filthy water over his face and neck. And he was still facing the opposite way when Max pulled the Ziploc bag from his pocket, filled it with water and sealed it. He walked back to the log pile, the bag of water hidden under his shirt.

'Ready?' he said to Sami.

Sami wiped the sweat from his brow, glanced nervously across the clearing and nodded. 'Ready,' he replied.

14

Fire

Carefully, Max laid the Ziploc bag on the ground behind the log pile. While Sami kept watch, Max scraped handfuls of dry moss and lichen from the bark of the felled trees with his fingernails. He collected some pieces of bark too, and some splinters of wood. He put these in neat piles next to the bag.

His next problem was where to position himself. He needed to be in the sunlight, but out of view of anybody else in the clearing who might become suspicious if they saw him. He reckoned the Blueshirts wouldn't be a problem. They were like zombies, the way they dug their pits without even looking up. It was the Redshirts and Blackshirts he had to avoid. If he crouched behind the log pile, he was completely out of sight, but he was also in the shade. He had to shift a little to the left, but that put him in the line of sight of part of the clearing. His only option was to crouch low and trust Sami to stand in front of him and keep watch while he continued to chop wood.

The bag was bulbous and still wet on the outside. He wiped it with his sleeve so that it wouldn't drip on the dry tinder. Then he squeezed it gently so the skin of the bag tightened, making it smooth and convex. Like a lens.

Now came the difficult part. It was a question, he decided, of holding the bag at just the right angle and at the perfect height above the tinder. He spent a full five minutes trying to do this, checking every few seconds that Sami wasn't trying to attract his attention, before deciding it was impossible. There was a faint patch on the ground where the water was refracting the sunlight, but he couldn't get a concentrated beam.

'*Put it down!*' Sami hissed suddenly. Max almost dropped the bag. He laid it gently on the ground so it didn't burst or tear, then he stood up just in time to see a Blackshirt marching towards them. Max quickly turned his back on the log pile so that he was facing the jungle. He pretended to be peeing, before looking over his shoulder, 'noticing' the Blackshirt and deciding it wasn't a good idea. The Blackshirt stormed up to him and started shouting something, pointing towards the steaming pit Max had already assumed was a latrine. Max hung his head apologetically. The Blackshirt grunted, shouted something at the other Blueshirts, who shrank back at the sound of his voice, and sauntered back to the centre of the clearing.

'It's not working,' Max hissed at Sami. 'I can't get it right.'

'Try again,' Sami said. His face was full of trust. 'I know you can do it.'

Max retook his position behind the log pile, picked up the water bag and started trying to get a beam again. He had to do it methodically, he decided. He put the bag by the tinder and rotated it 360 degrees. Nothing. He raised it a little and did the same. Nothing. Another inch . . .

There it was! A sudden spot of white light on the tinder. It disappeared almost immediately. Max adjusted the bag, trying to find the white spot again. Now he knew he could do it, the job was easier. The beam focused on the tinder again. Max kept his hands as still as possible. The beam needed to stay on the same point to build up the heat.

Five seconds passed.

Ten.

Thirty.

Sixty.

His hands were shaking. He took long, slow breaths to calm himself. Then, almost from nowhere, a thin tendril of smoke rose from the pile of lichen and dried moss. Max kept the beam on it for a few more seconds. The smoke grew thicker. He got in close and gently blew on the tinder to get some oxygen into the mix. He reached for the smallest shard of kindling he could find – it was little bigger than a needle – and laid it on the tinder. There was the tiniest, faintest crackle as the shard flamed like a match. Max took some more shards. He could hear Woody's voice during training back at Valley House. *Guys, remember. Look after a fire when it's small, it'll look after you when it's big . . .*

'Don't rush it,' Max muttered to himself. He knew that the best way to kill a fire was to add too much fuel too soon. He carefully fed the flames with tiny pieces of wood, increasing their size only when the fire was big enough to take it. Five minutes later, he had a decent blaze. The flames were a couple of hands high, and the fire was close enough to the log pile that the dry wood had started to catch. Max blew on it a little more. Then he emptied the Ziploc bag, shoved it in his pocket and went to re-join Sami.

Sami was sweating nervously. 'When do we raise the alarm?' he whispered as Max grabbed his axe and they both started chopping again.

'We don't,' Max said. 'Wait till it's big enough for them to notice by themselves. If we're going to get over to Babaka's hut, it's got to take up everyone's attention.' He glanced over at the Blueshirts, who were still digging.

It happened faster than Max had expected. The log pile was dry and the fuel it provided was plentiful. A few minutes later, there was a shout. A couple of Redshirts pointed at the log pile. All of a sudden, it was as if the whole camp knew what was happening. Max couldn't help a faint smile. Flames were licking up to the top of the pile, and the frame that covered it was ablaze. He and Sami stepped away from the fire, feigning surprise and fear. Even the other Blueshirts had noticed it now and were staring at it, looking uncertain. Should they run or stay where they were?

Max had correctly predicted that burning the camp's fuel supply would be a big deal. Within seconds, the Blackshirts were pointing and shouting, yelling for the Redshirts to grab any containers they could find and fetch water from the stream. One of the Blackshirts ran up to Max, Sami and the Blueshirts. He screamed at them and pointed towards the stream. His meaning was clear: *Get to work. Put this fire out.*

The Blueshirts started to jog across the clearing. Max and Sami joined them. They passed Redshirts coming the other way, carefully carrying water in all sorts of containers: cracked plastic buckets, tin cups, bamboo tubes. None of the containers held much water. Max noted with satisfaction that it would take a long time to extinguish the flames – if they managed it at all.

As he jogged, Max looked around. He glanced up at the plateau. Blackshirts were running down the steps to help extinguish the fire. He couldn't see Lukas. Babaka's hut was three along in the direction of Max's ten o'clock. He checked carefully for any sign of Babaka himself. There was none. 'I'm going,' he hissed at Sami. 'Stay with the other Blueshirts. They're more likely to notice if we're both missing.'

Sami nodded imperceptibly. They were by the nearest hut. Max made sure nobody was watching him. Everybody was focused on the fire. He slipped away from the line of Blueshirts and, with his back against the wall of the hut, edged round to its far side.

He was sweating. His heart thumped. People were shouting in alarm. He tried to zone them all out, to focus on his immediate surroundings and the path to Babaka's hut. To get there, first he had to cross open ground to another hut that stood between him and Babaka's. If anyone was watching from the plateau, they would see him.

But nobody was. Max checked left and right. *All clear.* He sprinted across the open ground and, breathless, hid in the shelter of the second hut.

He could see Babaka's place. Distance: eight or nine metres. From this angle, he could just see that the door was ajar. Max reckoned he could be in and out in less than a minute. But he had to choose his moment carefully. If anyone found him in there, he was a dead man.

He checked his surroundings again. To his left he could just make out the fire and the line of people rushing to put it out. To his right, the plateau. Up ahead, nothing. Instinct told him to wait, but logic disagreed. Nobody was watching him. The longer he left it, the greater the chance that the situation would change and someone would arrive. He wouldn't have a better chance than now.

He ran.

Halfway to Babaka's hut, he froze.

In front of him was Babaka. He had appeared from behind another hut and was hurrying towards his own. He hadn't spotted Max yet because he was looking back over his shoulder, shouting at somebody. As soon as he looked ahead, however, he'd see him.

It was as if Max was paralysed. He couldn't move. Although his brain shrieked at him to sprint back, his limbs wouldn't obey. Like a rabbit caught in headlights, he stared at Babaka, frozen to the spot, even as the Blackshirt started to turn his head . . .

To Max, it felt as though everything was happening in slow motion. Something flew through the air from the jungle. Max didn't realise it was a stone until it cracked Babaka in the head. He shouted in pain and covered his face with his hands. Suddenly Max's limbs were free. He turned and sprinted back to the first hut, hurling himself out of Babaka's sight.

He cursed under his breath. From here he could see that the log-pile fire was subsiding. Two Redshirts were moving the tank of putrid water Max had used to fill the Ziploc bag over to the flames. They tipped it onto the fire.

Max's stomach churned. After all that, he'd missed his chance. The Blackshirts ordered the Blueshirts back to work. Sami was with them, surreptitiously searching for Max, who jogged up to join him. 'Did you find it?' Sami whispered.

'I couldn't get in,' Max said. 'Babaka turned up. But listen, something really weird happened. He was about to catch me when someone threw a stone at his head.'

'Who?'

'I don't know. I didn't see them. But I think they must have been watching, because it came at just the right time.' They were back at the wood-chopping place along with all the other Blueshirts. A couple of Blackshirts were examining the charred woodpile, but there were no more flames. Max picked up his axe, pretending to get back to work. 'We haven't seen Roland in a while,' he said. 'I think it might have been him.'

'No,' Sami said. 'It wasn't Roland.'

'How do you know?'

He pointed back into the clearing. 'Look over there.'

Max looked at the entrance to the clearing. Two Blackshirts had emerged from the jungle, leading a prisoner by a rope around his neck. They were quite a distance from Max and Sami, but they could tell from the slouch of his body that he was exhausted, demoralised and possibly in pain.

They could also see that it was Roland.

Babaka strode up to Roland. The Blackshirt was clutching his face where the stone had hit him, and his anger exploded as soon as he reached the prisoner. He backhanded Roland across the cheek. Roland's knees buckled, but he wasn't allowed to fall to the ground. The Blackshirt holding the rope yanked him up by the neck. Babaka pointed in the direction of the plateau and Roland was led in that direction, towards Oscar Juwani's lair.

A strange silence fell over the camp. Everybody watched as the Blackshirts forced Roland up the stairs to the plateau. Max and Sami watched too. For the first time, Max thought he could see Lukas at the edge of the plateau, surveying the scene. Maybe he was searching for his former friends. Maybe he was doing something else. Max didn't know.

'What are they going to do to him?' Sami said.

'I don't want to think about it,' Max said. But he could think of little else. Roland was a good guy. He had helped them. It was up to them to help him, in whatever way they could.

He glanced over towards Babaka's hut. There was no chance of getting there now. There were too many people – Redshirts and Blackshirts – milling around. He couldn't help thinking about the stone again. It had come from nowhere, but surely it hadn't been a coincidence. Somebody had thrown it. Somebody who was trying to help Max.

And then he thought about last night, and the figure he had seen running around the clearing. A wild, impossible thought formed in his mind.

15

Genius

Lukas had not been allowed to move from the plateau outside Oscar Juwani's hut. He had not slept, and had eaten only a few mouthfuls of cold meat and congealed fat for breakfast. Nor had he been allowed to leave his position by the covered snake pit. He had grown used to the smell and the sound of the hissing from the black mambas, though it still made him shiver. He noticed that, as the sun grew higher, the slithering increased. He supposed that was because the snakes were warming up.

He knew Max and Sami had set the fire, though he wasn't sure how they'd managed it. As soon as he had seen the smoke billowing up from the far end of the clearing, he had been on high alert. He had watched carefully. Was he the only person who had seen Max slip from hut to hut, only to be repelled by Babaka's arrival at the last minute? Was he the only person who had seen the rock fly into Babaka's face? Was he the only one who knew who had thrown it? He couldn't tell. All he knew was, Max was surely attempting to get into Babaka's hut to find the watch. He had failed to do that. They were back to square one.

In fact, they were further back than that.

Then there was a commotion at the top of the stairs leading to the plateau. Several Blackshirts appeared, pulling Roland along. He was obviously terrified. Lukas felt a pang of remorse as Roland glanced at him, because the sight of Lukas seemed to make Roland doubly fearful. But it was nothing to his expression when Oscar Juwani appeared outside his hut. Amid the confusion, Lukas realised that Babaka was there, sidling up to Oscar Juwani. He muttered something to the cult leader and pointed at Roland. Roland, terrified though he obviously was, jutted his chin out in defiance. Oscar Juwani almost seemed to find that funny. He waddled over to Roland, held his prisoner's chin between his fat fingers and examined his face closely. Then he turned to Lukas. 'Do you know who this is, my friend?'

Lukas knew better than to lie, with Babaka standing close by. 'I recognise him,' he said.

'Is he a friend of yours?'

'No.'

'Good! That will make this so much easier for you.' He issued an instruction. Two of the Blackshirts hurried up to the snake pit. With obvious reluctance, they lifted the lid from the pit and laid it on the ground. Oscar Juwani nodded at the Blackshirt who was holding the rope around Roland's neck. The Blackshirt led Roland to one end of the pit. When he saw what was in there, he tried to run, but another Blackshirt was there to grab him by the shoulders and hold him still. The guy with the rope walked it round to the other end of the pit. Lukas noticed that he kept his distance from the edge. One good tug, however, and maybe a push from the Blackshirt holding him, and Roland would be dragged inside. The rope guy held it up and looked enquiringly at Oscar Juwani.

Oscar Juwani, however, was more interested in Lukas. He was staring carefully at him, as though judging his reaction. Lukas tried very hard not to give him one. He just stared straight ahead.

'This boy,' Oscar Juwani announced, 'is not a stranger to us. Did you know that, Lukas?'

Lukas didn't trust himself to reply.

'He was here some weeks ago, with his brother. For some reason, they did not find it convenient to stay. They tried to escape. His brother? Him, we found. He is no longer with us. This boy, on the other hand, eluded us until he was discovered prowling round our camp. No doubt he was to blame for our little fire. I can only think that he wished to do us harm, so I regret a punishment is necessary.'

Roland was sweating and trembling. His eyes were continuously drawn to the seething, hissing contents of the pit. Every time he saw inside, he recoiled and turned his head. But then he would look again, drawn back to the horror.

'Perhaps, Lukas,' Oscar Juwani said, 'this could be a good job for you. Perhaps this is an opportunity for you to earn yourself a black shirt.'

Lukas felt his jaw clench. He didn't – couldn't – reply.

'Yes,' Oscar Juwani said. 'Yes, I think that is a good idea. Take the rope. Finish the job for us.'

There was silence. Nobody moved apart from Roland, who was trembling violently. Lukas could feel everybody staring at him.

'Come along, Lukas,' Oscar Juwani wheezed. 'Show us how keen you are to be one of us.'

Nobody moved. Lukas could barely breathe. He swallowed hard and glanced towards the steps. Maybe, if he made a run for it that way . . . But no. The stairs were guarded. He glanced left, towards the jungle at the back of the plateau. To run that way meant getting past at least three Blackshirts. And if they caught him, which they would, he knew what would happen. As if to confirm it, there was a crescendo of hissing from the pit.

'What is it, Lukas?' Oscar Juwani said. 'Is Babaka right? Are you not as loyal as you pretend?' He was not smiling any more. 'Do it.'

Slowly, Lukas walked to the end of the pit opposite Roland. Now that he was close, he could see inside more clearly than he had last night. The snakes were a black, knotted mess in slow but constant motion. The smell was foul. Lukas looked away as he approached the Blackshirt who was holding the rope. With an unpleasant grin, the Blackshirt handed the rope to Lukas, then stepped away. Lukas gripped the rope firmly. There was not much slack. One good tug and Roland would be in the pit. Roland's expression silently implored Lukas not to do as Oscar Juwani was urging him.

Lukas glanced around. The Blackshirts were grinning. All except Babaka, who to Lukas's surprise was frowning. They were all armed, but they were enjoying the show too much to have their weapons primed. Instead, their rifles hung loosely across their backs, barrels up, or their chests, barrels down.

Maybe, Lukas thought, that gave him a chance.

Oscar Juwani was about ten paces away. Lukas estimated that he could get to him in two seconds, if he really moved. And if the rope was long enough. If he could wrap it around Oscar Juwani's neck, and pull tight before the Blackshirts had time to engage their weapons, maybe he had a chance. Would Oscar Juwani call off his guys if he risked being throttled or even hurled into the pit? Lukas thought he might. In any case, this was his – and Roland's – only chance.

He pulled on the rope a little. Where it had been lying across the top of the pit, it now hung in mid-air. Lukas had some slack. With the leading end of the rope in his left hand, he held it half a metre further along with his right. Roland struggled. He obviously thought he was about to be tugged into the pit. The Blackshirt behind him held him fast.

Lukas glanced over at Oscar Juwani. He breathed deeply and prepared to sprint in that direction in three . . .

Two . . .

One . . .

'What is it, Babaka?'

Lukas froze. Babaka had said something. Oscar Juwani, looking irritated, was telling him to elaborate. Babaka spoke. Lukas didn't understand a word. When Babaka fell silent, Oscar Juwani seemed to be pondering his words. 'Very well,' he murmured. 'Maybe Babaka is right.'

'What?' Lukas said.

'The young man who killed this one's brother is an eager Redshirt. He is out in the jungle. We expect him back tonight. If there is another killing to be done, Babaka believes he deserves the chance to do it and earn himself a black shirt.' Oscar Juwani smiled. 'Of course, you are not stupid, are you, Lukas? You can tell that Babaka is not your greatest fan. Perhaps he is only saying this because he does not want you to earn yourself a black shirt. What do you think of that?'

Lukas had the presence of mind to shrug, as if he didn't care either way. He pointed at Roland. 'This one, another one,' he said. 'It makes no difference to me.' He slung the rope back across the pit, where it coiled at Roland's feet. Oscar Juwani nodded slowly and barked a command. Two Blackshirts covered the pit and pulled Roland away from the edge. His hands and legs were tied and he was forced to lie on his front.

'We will deal with him at first light tomorrow,' Oscar Juwani announced. Then he waddled back into his hut and his Blackshirt guards took up their position by the door.

Lukas wanted to speak to Roland. To tell him not to panic. To tell him he would never have tugged him into the pit, and that he would do everything in his power to make sure it didn't happen in the morning. But he did not dare, under Babaka's watchful gaze. Anyway, he didn't know what promises he could make.

So Lukas returned to his position by the snake pit and did the only thing he could. He waited until nightfall. He waited for help.

Down in the clearing, the sun was sinking fast. But not as fast as Max's hopes. He'd had one chance to capitalise on their distraction, and he'd blown it. Two Blackshirts stood by the log pile, so there was no chance of a repeat performance with the Ziploc bag. Max and Sami were exhausted, demoralised and scared. To make things worse, a troop of mischievous monkeys were pelting them with nuts and berries. In another time and place, it would have been funny. But the missiles were hard, and they hurt.

Max and Sami's skin was already sore from insect bites and jungle cuts. They swore as they struggled to chop the wood, their muscles burning and their hearts anxious.

'What do you think happened to Roland?' Sami whispered when the Blackshirts weren't watching.

'I don't know,' Max said. 'Something was going on up there a while back, but –' he shrugged – 'I couldn't tell what. Ow!' Something hit him hard in the face. 'Stupid monkeys,' he hissed. 'I'd like to . . .'

He fell silent. The thing that had hit him on the face had fallen to the ground right in front of him. It was not a nut or a berry. It was metallic and colourful. He checked the Blackshirts weren't watching, then bent down to pick it up. He caught his breath. 'Sami, check this out!'

The item in his hand had once been circular. Now it had a well in the middle where something had struck it, leaving an indentation. It was a Special Forces Cadet challenge coin, warped by a bullet.

Max and Sami stared at each other. Suddenly everything made sense. The sensation of being followed through the jungle. The face he had seen by the track. The figure he had recognised running around the clearing. The stone that had hit Babaka. Max smiled. 'You genius, Lukas,' he whispered. 'You absolute genius.'

16

Piercings

Lili had once heard of an ancient form of torture: death by a thousand cuts. Now she and Abby felt as though they were suffering exactly that.

Following Max, Sami, Lukas and the others through the jungle had been difficult enough. The convoy had cleared a path for them, sure, but they had the horrific bruises on their chests to contend with. The challenge coins, with their Kevlar backing, had stopped the bullets from penetrating further. But the impact had still been enough to knock them over. The bruise had spread all the way up to Lili's shoulder, and she thought she might have a broken rib or two. It was probably that, she and Abby had decided, that had saved them. It was only in the seconds before Lukas had taken the shots that they had realised what his plan was. They had pushed out their chests so the shape of the challenge coins sewn into their shirts was visible, giving him a target. But they were in so much pain that they could barely move when they hit the ground. They *looked* dead, so the thugs assumed they were dead. It was only afterwards that they could marvel at the accuracy of Lukas's shooting, and at his quick thinking.

The bruises had grown worse as the hours passed. Breathing was painful. But that wasn't their only problem. It felt as if the jungle was reaching out to tear at their skin. The vegetation around the clearing where the others had been taken was unusually thick. No doubt, Lili thought, Oscar Juwani had chosen it for that reason. Moving through it tore their clothes and their skin. At one point last night, as they kept a careful watch over the clearing, Abby had even risked running from one vantage point to another along the perimeter. Lili had been angry with her, but Abby was in a worse state than her friend. Her face was scratched and bloody, her skin puffy and her eyes bloodshot. It hadn't dulled her wits though. It was Abby who'd had the presence of mind to throw the rock at Babaka – 'I've always liked a good game of rounders,' she'd whispered as the rock cracked into the Blackshirt's head – and it was Abby's plan to chuck the warped challenge coin at Max and Sami. 'They'll know what it means,' she'd said. 'They're cleverer than they look. Well, they'd have to be, really, don't you think?'

Abby was right. Hiding behind the treeline, they could see Max and Sami. Max was turning the challenge coin over in his fingers, staring up at the plateau where Lukas was being held. Then he stared back into the jungle, as though trying to penetrate the trees, searching and scanning. They saw him mouth the words 'Abby' and 'Lili' – silent confirmation that he knew they were there.

One of the Blackshirts shouted at them. Max and Sami went back to chopping wood. They seemed less exhausted. As if their new discovery had given them hope.

Lili and Abby retreated from the treeline, deeper into the jungle. 'Did you see Max's face?' Abby said, her voice cracking because her throat was so dry. 'Not going to lie, that was sweet.'

Lili gave her an irritated frown. 'We have work to do,' she said.

'You mean I can't go sunbathing?'

'Seriously, Abby. We've left this too long already. Roland has been captured. Who knows if those SAS men are still alive? And it's only a matter of time before they force Lukas into a killing that he can't get out of. Come on, let's recap what we know.'

'Lili, we've recapped what we know about ten times already.'

'Well, we're going to recap again.' Lili frowned. 'We think Max is trying to get into Babaka's hut. The only reason we can think of is to get at the watch. It's a good job we spent last night watching the clearing. We know that Lukas is being kept outside Oscar Juwani's hut on the plateau. We know that Max and Sami will probably spend tonight back in that bamboo cage. We know that at any time during the night there are three Blackshirts patrolling the clearing. One walks the perimeter, another walks the length of the clearing, and a third walks its width. About every forty-five minutes the perimeter guy and the length guy meet by the log pile, where they normally stop for a couple of minutes to smoke a cigarette. At the same time, the width guy is at the far side of the clearing. If we want to get Max and Sami out of the cage, that's the time to do it.'

Abby shook her head. 'I don't know, Lili,' she said, her voice more serious. 'It seems risky to me. If we know the watch is in Babaka's hut, why don't we just get in there ourselves?'

'Because that won't work,' Lili said. 'It will need more than two of us. One to enter the hut, one to keep watch outside it, but also one or two of us to distract the patrolling Blackshirts, especially the guy making his way back from the far side.'

'You've got it all worked out,' Abby said.

'Not all of it,' Lili said. 'We still don't know how we're going to break Max and Sami out of the cage. The door is chained shut and there's a big padlock.'

'Don't you worry about that,' Abby said. 'I was born in a prison, remember? I learned to pick locks in there before I learned to read. I've never met a padlock I couldn't open.'

'What will you use?'

Abby smiled enigmatically. She put her hand to her right

ear and removed one of her elaborate cartilage piercings. She straightened out the metal so that it resembled a wonky, unfurled paper clip. Then she held it up. Lili had one eyebrow raised.

'What?' Abby said. 'I like to accessorise, okay?' She put the earring in her pocket. 'Max and Sami can buy me some new ones when we get back home.'

'If we get back home,' Lili said.

'No,' Abby replied. '*When* we get back home. What's the plan?'

'We wait till nightfall,' Lili said. 'We keep watch on the guards and when everything's quiet we choose our moment. We cross the clearing to the cage, where we unlock the padlock and let Max and Sami out. They get to Babaka's hut and try to activate the watch. We hide among the other huts and, if we need to, we make a noise to distract the guards. If – I mean, *when* – Max and Sami have activated the watch, we lock them back in the cage so nobody notices they've gone and raises the alarm. We hide back in the jungle and wait for the Watchers to arrive and get us and the SAS team out of here.'

'You make it sound so easy,' Abby said.

Lili ignored that. 'I wish we could get a message to Max and Sami,' she said. 'To tell them what we're planning.'

'They'll be expecting us,' Abby said. 'They know that tonight's our last chance. If we leave it any longer, the SAS guys will likely be dead and Lukas will be in a situation he can't get himself out of. Come on, let's find a place to lie, as close to Max and Sami's cage as we can get. It's going to be a long night. We'll need all our strength.'

When the light failed and they could no longer see to chop, Max, Sami and the other Blueshirts were given scraps of food. It was a pungent dried meat that Max couldn't identify and would never have touched had he not been ravenous. But he was, so he ate it gratefully, as did Sami. Then they were led back to the cage and locked inside.

The kid with the sore hands lay down immediately. Max felt his temperature: he was burning hot. Max wasn't sure that he would last the night. Somehow that, more even than the thought of the SAS men in the cage or their own predicament, made Max determined that they had to make a move tonight, for better or worse. The other Blueshirts were asleep within minutes. Max and Sami sat by the door. Max felt physically exhausted but mentally sharp. The sight of the challenge coin, warped and battered, had reinvigorated him.

'Lukas was very clever,' Sami said quietly. 'Do you remember how he asked for a pistol instead of an assault rifle? The Kevlar on the challenge coin would never have stopped an assault rifle round. But with the 9mm from the pistol, he knew he had a chance.'

Max nodded. 'And Abby and Lili must have known what he was going to do,' he said. 'Do you remember how they pushed their chests out? That made the coins more visible. Still, he made two great shots. Even Hector would have been impressed.'

'Hector? Impressed? Well, maybe.' Sami stared over to the edge of the clearing. 'Do you think Abby and Lili are watching us?'

'I'm certain of it,' Max said. 'My guess is they spent last night putting in surveillance. They'll know the movements of the guards and they'll be biding their time. Either they'll try to get into Babaka's place by themselves, or they'll try to get us out of the cage and we'll do it together. Either way, it'll happen tonight.'

'What about Lukas?'

Max flinched. His elation at learning about Lukas's cleverness had faded a little. He felt guilty at the way he had treated his friend. At his inability to be as trusting of him as Sami had been. 'I don't know,' Max said quietly. 'My guess is he's too heavily guarded up there on the plateau to be of any help. And if we want to help him . . .'

'Our best bet is to call in the Watchers,' Sami completed the sentence for him. He frowned at Max. 'He will understand why you spoke to him the way you did,' he said.

'I hope so,' Max said. He glanced up at the plateau. 'I hope he's okay up there. I hope they don't make him *do* anything . . .' He shook his head, unable to finish the thought. 'We should get our heads down,' he said. 'If the guards think we're sleeping, they'll take less interest in us. And we definitely want them to take less interest in us.'

Sami nodded fervently and lay down. Max did the same. Lying on his side, he looked out towards the jungle. It was almost dark, and it was impossible to see any distance beyond the treeline. But Max didn't need to do that. Somehow, he knew – he just *knew* – that two Special Forces Cadets were out there in the jungle. They were watching him and Sami, and waiting for their moment.

17

1, 2, 3

'Ah, it's okay for some,' Abby said, 'having a spot of supper and a nice lie-down.'

'Are you always this sarcastic?' Lili said, a little irritably.

'Only when I'm hungry.'

'You're always hungry, Abby.'

'Aren't I though?'

They crouched behind a shield of broad palm leaves, watching the clearing through the gaps made by the fronds. Max and Sami's cage was about seventy-five metres away, Lili estimated. She wasn't going to lie to herself. It looked like a long seventy-five metres. She squinted through the darkness. She had the uncanny sense that Max was staring straight at them. It made her want to hide deeper in the jungle. 'We stay hidden till about midnight,' she told Abby. 'Then we check the position of the guards.'

They could only estimate the time. It passed slowly as they crouched in the pitch-black jungle, jumping at every sound. Abby didn't even complain about being hungry – a sure sign that she was anxious, because they had not eaten since they were in the village, and the only water they had found had been condensation on broad green jungle leaves. It was a relief when she finally said, 'Hey, Lili, it's got to be about time, right?'

'Right,' Lili whispered. 'Let's check the guards.'

They edged back to the treeline and scanned the clearing. The fires had burned low. Their embers still glowed, however, and a few people moved about. Lili turned her attention to the guards. In her mind she had labelled them. Guard 1 was walking the perimeter of the clearing, Guard 2 was walking its length and Guard 3 its width. They needed to wait until Guards 1 and 2 met by the log pile and stopped for their cigarette and Guard 3 was at the far side of the clearing. That moment had just passed. Guard 2 had just set off from the log pile, walking left to right. Guard 3 was heading towards them, almost alongside the cage. Guard 2 was on the far side of the clearing, walking the perimeter.

'It's going to be another half hour, at least,' Lili said.

They waited, motionless. Guard 3 approached them. He stopped at the edge of the clearing, close enough to Abby and Lili that they could smell him: woodsmoke and body odour. The guard peered unseeingly into the jungle while Abby and Lili held their breath. He turned and started marching back across the clearing. 'He can be *your* boyfriend,' Abby whispered.

Lili didn't reply. She was too firmly focused on the

guards. Carefully she watched them walking up and down, left and right, round and round, waiting for that precise, magic instant when they were all as far away as they could be, and distracted.

It happened around forty-five minutes later. Guards 1 and 2 stopped by the log pile for their cigarette. Guard 3 was at the far side of the clearing. They had to move now, or not at all.

'Go!' Lili hissed. '*Go!*'

They emerged silently from the jungle and sprinted across the open ground, crouched low, towards the cage. As they approached, Lili saw Max and Sami sit up. Her eyes panned left and right, searching, checking that nobody else in the slumbering camp had seen them. They seemed to be safe.

Then they were by the cage. None of the other Blueshirts were awake, but Max and Sami peered out anxiously from behind the bamboo bars.

'Surprise!' Abby whispered, even though they didn't seem surprised at all.

'What kept you?' Max breathed.

'You'd better be nice to me, Maxy baby, otherwise I might decide not to let you out of this funny little cage.' Even as she spoke, however, she pulled out her earring and went to work on the padlock. Her boasts hadn't been idle. She had it open in seconds.

'Has anyone seen Lukas?' Max whispered as Abby quickly and quietly undid the chain.

'Not since last night,' Lili said.

'Roland . . .' Sami started to say.

'We know. Guys, we have to activate that watch.'

'We think it's in Babaka's hut,' Max said.

'Right,' Lili said. 'You and Sami go get it. We'll distract any guards if we need to.'

'By throwing rocks in their faces?'

'We might need to be a bit more subtle this time.'

The cage was open. Max and Sami stepped out.

'Chain it up again,' Max said. 'Otherwise it'll attract attention. But don't lock the padlock. When we've activated the GPS signal, we'll get back in the cage and wait for the Watchers to get here. You two will need to go back into the jungle.'

'Okay,' Lili said. She nodded towards Guards 1 and 2, who were stubbing out their cigarettes. 'Go!' she hissed. '*Go!*'

A part of Max wished he was back in the cage. There, he would at least be safe and undisturbed until morning. Another part of him knew that this was exactly how Oscar Juwani wanted him: subdued and fearful. Passive. It was the first step on the path to being completely controlled.

Which wasn't going to happen.

He and Sami ran to the hut nearest the cage. They pressed against the wall and waited in the shadows. The guard patrolling the length of the clearing was approaching.

He was about thirty metres away. Slowly they edged round to the other side of the hut, where they could wait for him to pass without him seeing them. Max's palms were clammy, his jugular pulsing. He heard the guard humming tunelessly to himself as he passed nearby. And as the humming faded, he focused on the path to Babaka's hut. There were three other huts between them. Distance between each hut: approximately fifteen metres.

'Go!' he whispered to Sami. Together they crossed to the first of the three huts, and took refuge once again in the shadow of its exterior wall.

Max checked back the way they had come. He could see the guard walking towards the far end of the clearing. He also saw a dark figure flit between two huts. It reminded him of catching a glimpse of a bat flying against the night sky. He knew it was Lili or Abby following the guard, ready to distract him if necessary.

But they had to move again. The other guard, the one patrolling the width of the clearing, was close. Too close. They could hear his footsteps. As they edged round the hut, he appeared to their right. They froze. To Max's horror, the guard started to turn to his left. He was going to spot them any second . . .

A noise. A throaty kind of screech. Was it an animal? Or was it, as Max suspected, one of the girls? Whatever, whoever, it was, it distracted the guard, and he carried on walking across the clearing.

Silence. Max and Sami moved to the second hut, then the third. Here they had to wait in the shadows once more. The guard at the perimeter had stopped and was staring curiously in their direction. Then he shook his head and continued his patrol.

The coast was clear. Or as clear as it would ever be. Babaka's hut was ten metres away. But there was a problem. The door was ajar, and a faint, flickering light glowed inside. Maybe a candle. Cursing himself, Max realised he hadn't even considered the possibility that Babaka would still be awake.

'We can't go in,' Sami said, so quietly that Max could barely make out his words. 'If he sees us, we'll never get another chance to –'

'Wait there,' Max breathed. He knew they couldn't delay. After another night, there was every chance that the SAS men and Roland would be dead. 'Make a bird sound or something if anyone comes.'

'But, Max . . .'

Max didn't wait. Quickly and silently he crossed over to Babaka's hut, where he stood with his back to the wall, next to the open door.

He listened intently. There was no sound of movement. But there was, he thought, the sound of heavy, regular breathing. Not snoring exactly, but definitely the noise people made when they were asleep. He glanced at Sami, who was staring at him in alarm. Then – carefully, and infinitely slowly – he pushed the door open a little wider.

He looked inside.

Babaka's hut was sparse. There was an old mattress resting on a bed frame made of logs. No sheets. Next to it, a three-legged stool. On the stool was a candle, short, stubby and guttering. Babaka was lying on the bed, his eyes closed, his mouth open, his chest softly rising and falling. He was definitely asleep. Max noticed a poster on the wall: Lionel Messi. It seemed bizarre that Babaka should be interested in something so normal as football. Max reminded himself that Babaka was, under it all, a teenager like him. Well, maybe not *quite* like him. Babaka lay on his back, his submachine gun next to him. His left arm lay protectively over his weapon. His right hung over the side of the bed. The watch was around his wrist. Babaka had put it back on.

Great, Max thought. Now what? He checked over his shoulder. Sami was silently, but furiously, gesturing at him to get out. Max turned back to the hut. He had already made his decision. He knew it was risky, but he also knew that if they didn't take a few risks, they'd never escape. And he might not get another chance like this.

He stepped into the hut. The thick silence seemed to amplify his every move. As he stepped towards the sleeping man, he was acutely aware of his footsteps, and of the sound of his trousers brushing together, and of his heart.

He wanted to move fast, to be out of there as quickly as possible. But he forced himself to be slow, to avoid waking his enemy.

Three paces.

Five.

He was by the bed. Babaka hadn't stirred. Max knelt, wincing at the rustle of his trousers. He was so close to the watch, and he had a decision to make. Should he activate the PLB while it was still on Babaka's wrist? Or should he remove the watch first?

He decided he had to remove the watch. Once the PLB was activated, the antenna would be visible, and the game would be up. His hands shook. He breathed deeply to steady them. Then, gingerly, he felt for the clasp on the underside of Babaka's wrist.

His fingertips touched the metal.

Babaka stirred.

Max jumped. Babaka rolled over and his watch hand almost hit Max in the face. He lay facing away from Max, his watch hand draped over the other side of the bed.

Silently, Max cursed. He stood up. His shadow, long and flickering in the candlelight, darkened Babaka and the floor and wall beyond him. Stealthily, Max moved round the bed and crouched down. He reached out for the clasp. Touched it.

Babaka's eyes flickered open.

18

PLB

Max froze. Babaka's hand shot out and he grabbed Max by the throat. His big hand squeezed Max's carotid artery. A sharp pain cracked through his neck. He tried to breathe. It was impossible.

Still clutching Max's neck, Babaka sat up. The submachine gun was lying on the mattress. With an almost inhuman snarl, Babaka grabbed the weapon with his free hand. Max thought he was going to fire at him from point-blank range. But then he saw that the Blackshirt was not holding the weapon in the ordinary way. He was clutching the stock and raising it to use as a bludgeon.

Max raised his left arm to ward off the blow. He hissed with pain as the weapon struck his forearm, but managed to clench his right fist and thump Babaka in the side of the face. Max was strong, but it was as if Babaka was made of iron. Max's fist practically bounced off him. Max went for another punch as Babaka raised the weapon again. Max aimed his fist directly at Babaka's nose, hoping to break it. But he was concentrating so much on that manoeuvre that he failed to protect himself. The gun cracked against the left side of his face. White-hot agony shot through him and he felt the slow, warm ooze of blood trickling from his nostrils. He fell to the ground, stunned. He tried to grab Babaka's ankles, but Babaka's hand was around his neck again, pulling him up to his feet, pushing him against the wall of the hut. Babaka was muttering something, his voice a growl. He sneered again, then brought his knee up hard into Max's stomach. Max doubled over, gasping for breath. Then he felt the bony impact of Babaka's knee again, this time cracking into Max's chin. His head swung back, and blood sprayed from his nose.

Everything spun. Max fought to stay conscious. Not easy. He had an urge to vomit, and it took all his effort to remain standing. Babaka was shouting – screaming, in fact, at the top of his voice, raising the alarm. Other voices, from all over the camp, joined in. Max zoomed his attention back to Babaka. He had Max by the throat again. The wristwatch was only inches from Max's chin. Max knew he had a chance. He raised his right arm – it was shaking and weak – towards the watch. If he could just reach it, he could activate the GPS signal . . .

But Babaka was throttling him. His fierce expression told Max he was enjoying it. The Blackshirt stared into Max's face as though waiting for the light to leave

Max's eyes. It meant he wasn't paying any attention to Max's hands. Max's fingertips were almost touching the watch . . .

Suddenly Babaka pulled Max away from the wall and hurled him across the hut. Max stumbled over a corner of the bed and collapsed. Babaka engaged his weapon, pointed it directly at Max and made a 'get up' motion with the gun. Max forced himself painfully to his feet. Babaka gestured. His meaning was clear: *get outside.*

There was a good deal of noise in the clearing. People were awake and moving around, on high alert. Max's thoughts turned to the others. Were they safe? Had they been captured? Had Max messed things up for all of them?

He had his answer as soon as he stepped out of the hut.

There were three Blackshirts immediately ahead of him. Two of them held burning branches to give them some light. One of them had Sami. He clutched Sami's hair with one hand. The other hand held a knife, pressed close to Sami's throat.

'*No!*' Max screamed, attempting to lunge at them. Babaka was close behind him however. He grabbed Max's own hair before he could take a step, and threw him to the ground once more. As Max hit the hard earth, the man with the knife spat at him. Babaka pointed in the direction of Oscar Juwani's plateau. The knife guy spun Sami around and started to frogmarch him across the clearing. Beyond him, Max could see more people, including two figures who were struggling. His heart sank. Was it Abby and Lili? If so, the guards had caught them and were leading them, along with Sami, up to the plateau.

Every cell in Max's body burned with panic. His head and stomach ached atrociously. He wanted to curl up on the ground to protect himself from any further beatings. But he also knew that this was his last chance. The Special Forces Cadets were blown. Captured. Their lives were at risk. If Max didn't call in the cavalry – immediately – their chances of survival were zero.

Babaka loomed over him, his submachine gun in his hand and contempt on his face. He gestured at Max to get up. At first Max pretended to be doing just that. Wincing dramatically, he pushed himself onto his knees. He straightened his back.

Then he struck.

He lunged at Babaka with all the momentum he could muster. He wrapped his arms tightly around the Blackshirt's knees and yanked his feet from under him by pushing one shoulder hard against his thighs.

Babaka was not expecting the attack. He collapsed, the back of his head thumping against the ground. As he fell, his finger slipped. A blistering line of rounds burst into the ground, inches from Max's leg. He felt the dirt exploding over him. He reached up with his right hand and knocked the MP5's safety switch into place. It wouldn't stop Babaka turning it back to automatic, but it would buy Max a couple of seconds.

Babaka still seemed stunned by the fall. Max took advantage of that. He clambered over the Blackshirt, landing heavily, his knees on Babaka's left arm.

The arm that had the watch.

Now was not the time for stealth or subtlety. Max grabbed Babaka's wrist with one hand. With the other, he felt for the dial on the side of the watch. All of a sudden, Babaka was writhing and roaring with rage. Max heard the safety switch clicking on the MP5. He knew he only had seconds. He dug his dirty, torn fingernails into the gap between the dial and the watch face. And as soon as he had a little purchase, he pulled.

The personal locator beacon was a thin wire, about thirty centimetres long. As Max tugged it from the watch, there was no indication that the GPS signal had been activated. No lights, no beeping. Just a length of wire flopping from the watch's body. Max couldn't examine it any further. Babaka smashed his gun against Max's side, knocking him to the ground again. As he fell, he managed to unclasp the watch from Babaka's wrist and pull it off. Babaka was so enraged, he didn't even seem to notice. The Blackshirt pushed himself to his feet. As he hulked over Max, he trod on the watch. To Max's horror, it shattered underfoot. Babaka pointed the MP5 at Max's head. His finger moved from the trigger guard to the trigger. Max knew he was about to fire.

So this was it. All he could do was hope that he had raised the alarm in time to save the others . . .

He closed his eyes and waited for the shots.

They didn't come.

Instead, there was a voice, low and harsh. Max opened his eyes again. The first thing he saw was Babaka lowering his weapon. Then he saw the man who had spoken. He was flanked by two armed guards and was immensely fat, with scars on his face and one milky eye. Max noticed in the moonlight that he was sweating heavily. He had a lit cigarette in one hand and was wearing military camouflage. He wheezed as he walked up to Max.

'Good evening, young man,' he said. And, when Max didn't reply, 'I assume you are a friend of Lukas. I must say, for a while he had me fooled. And it is not an easy thing to fool Oscar Juwani. But the idiotic actions of you and your other companions this evening have blown his cover, I'm afraid. I really should have listened to Babaka. He mistrusted you from the beginning. But it doesn't matter. We shall put an end to your games very quickly.'

Oscar Juwani nodded at Babaka, who yanked Max to his feet again. Then Juwani turned and, still accompanied by his two guards, walked across the clearing towards the plateau. Babaka poked his MP5 between Max's shoulder blades and nudged him forward. Max stumbled ahead, but as he moved he glanced back. The watch, crushed and broken, was still on the ground, the PLB snaking away from it. In the struggle, Babaka seemed to have forgotten all about it. He jabbed the barrel of the gun between Max's shoulder blades again. Up ahead, Max could see Sami, Lili and Abby being forced up the steps leading to the plateau.

He had no option but to follow.

19

Coward

Max knew that a fire burned constantly up here on the plateau. Over the past two days he had watched it from the clearing. Sometimes it smoked lazily. At other times it was fierce and hot. This was one of those times. It had obviously been newly stoked. Flames licked high and radiated a tremendous heat. Nobody stood closer than five metres to it, and most were further away than that. But the fire gave off as much light as it did heat, so as Babaka forced Max across the plateau, he was able to take everything in.

Eight Blackshirts stood there, all armed. Six had their weapons pointed at Lukas, Sami, Abby and Lili, who were kneeling along the far edge of a rectangular pit, their hands behind their backs. Their faces glowed and the reflection of the fire danced in their eyes. They were sweating. The six armed Blackshirts were behind them, their backs to the jungle. At the left-hand end of the pit, Roland was on his knees. Behind him stood Oscar Juwani, his smile fat and toad-like. He had his hands out, palms upwards. Had it not been for his camouflage gear, Max would have thought he looked like a priest about to administer a sacred rite. The sight made him shiver. Three people stood behind Oscar Juwani: the two Blackshirts who had guarded him, and a young man in a red shirt with a piercing on his upper lip.

Elsewhere on the plateau, to Max's right as he approached the pit, was a small crowd of Redshirts and Blueshirts. Their faces were indistinct in the darkness. There was a low-level hubbub as a few of them spoke in low voices. All Max's attention was on the pit. He didn't know what it contained, but he could tell that the other cadets were scared of it. As Babaka forced Max closer, he smelled a terrible stench. The smell of something rotting. It turned his stomach. Every muscle in his body wanted to resist approaching the pit, but that was not an option. He felt the MP5 poke him in the back again. He stumbled forward. Seconds later he was at the edge of the pit, on the opposite side to the other cadets. He could hear an angry hissing.

'Oh man,' he whispered. 'Not sn—'

'*Silence!*' Oscar Juwani's hiss was as sibilant as the sound from the pit.

The crowd of Redshirts and Blueshirts immediately fell silent. Nobody around the pit dared to speak. The fire crackled. Max could feel its heat on his back. Oscar Juwani licked his lips a little, then spoke again. 'I don't know who you are,' he said, 'and I don't really care. After tonight, you will no longer be a concern of mine.' He inhaled deeply. It was as if he liked the stench from the pit and wanted to get a lungful. 'My Blackshirts are all keen to kill you. They have been well schooled, and they would like to practise their weapons training with real targets. But special prisoners deserve special treatment, wouldn't you say?' He spread out his hands to indicate the pit. 'Anyway, we have Redshirts who are eager for promotion. What a shame it would be to deny them this opportunity.'

Oscar Juwani stepped aside and turned. The Redshirt with the lip ring was just behind him. Juwani took him by the arm and brought him closer to the end of the pit. The Redshirt's expression was dead. It reminded Max of Babaka. He was staring vacantly – not at the cadets, but at Roland. It looked as if Roland could feel the Redshirt's eyes burning into the back of his head. He was breathing heavily and looked terrified. Oscar Juwani said something to the Redshirt. The Redshirt started to talk quickly, his voice high-pitched and excited. Oscar Juwani translated. 'This excellent young man is called Katva. A few weeks ago, we had some guests who decided they did not want to stay with us. I'm afraid this is not something we like to encourage. One of these young men was this one.' He pointed at Roland. 'How nice it is to have him back here. The other was his brother – I'm afraid I forget his name.'

'His name,' Roland hissed, 'was Anton.'

'Is that so?' Oscar Juwani said. He clearly didn't like being interrupted. 'Well, it doesn't matter, does it?'

'His name,' Roland repeated, 'was Anton.'

'*Silence!*' Oscar Juwani spat. The hissing of the snakes in the pit swelled. Oscar Juwani composed himself before continuing. 'This one escaped. But young Katva managed to find his brother in the jungle. That is his speciality. He brought him back to us and executed him in return for a red shirt. Now, though, I think the time is right for Katva to earn himself a black shirt. Katva, show us what happens to anybody who tries to escape from our happy little camp.'

He clapped his hands, then repeated the instruction in his own language. Katva walked slowly up to Roland. He bent down and whispered something in his ear. Roland didn't move, so Katva grabbed his hair and dragged him to his feet. Roland's eyes darted left and right, as if he was searching for an escape route. But there was none. A couple of the Blackshirts had their weapons trained on him. Katva stood behind him and forced him to the edge of the pit. Roland teetered and Max thought he was going to fall. Katva held him back. Max could tell that the Redshirt was enjoying this, and was deliberately prolonging Roland's agony.

The flames behind Max licked even higher. It was uncomfortably hot and the sudden surge sounded like it had encouraged more activity in the snake pit. Long shadows, cast by the firelight, flickered towards the thick curtain of foliage at the back of the plateau. As it did so, Max thought he saw movement in the jungle. Was it the Watchers? Had they arrived? That thought died as soon as it arrived in his head. He had only activated the PLB ten minutes ago. That was surely not enough time. And anyway, the movement had stopped. Perhaps he had imagined it.

Roland suddenly let out a sob. It made the Blackshirts laugh. Oscar Juwani smiled grotesquely, and he gave an instruction that Max took to mean: 'Do it!'

'Wait!'

It was Sami, who was still kneeling with the others on the far side of the pit. His voice was loud and authoritative. It silenced everybody. Oscar Juwani showed a flicker of annoyance. He clenched his fists, then relaxed them. 'What is it, young man?' he said, his voice dangerously low.

'I think you're a coward,' Sami said. His accusation rang across the clearing. Nobody spoke.

Oscar Juwani inclined his head, as though stretching out a tight muscle in his neck. 'Is that so?' he replied.

'Yes,' Sami said, nodding his head firmly. 'That is so.'

'Sami,' Max hissed, 'don't wind him up.'

But Sami ignored him. 'Would you like to know why?' he said.

'I think we would all like to know why,' Oscar Juwani said smoothly, indicating everyone on the plateau, although few of them spoke English.

'Because you get other people to do your dirty work for you. And not just any old people. Young people. Children. You bully them because they can't fight back, and because you're too weak to stand up to people your own size.' Sami shook his head. 'It's not right. You should be prepared to do your own work and accept the consequences. You don't. That's why you are a coward.'

Nobody spoke. Even the snakes seemed quieter. Oscar Juwani stared at Sami. They *all* stared at Sami: the Blackshirts around the pit and the Redshirts and Blueshirts watching from elsewhere on the plateau. The other cadets looked aghast. What was Sami doing? Why would he antagonise Oscar Juwani like this? There was something else going on here, Max thought. There had to be. Sami wasn't stupid. He had a plan, though what that plan could be, Max didn't know. But whatever it was, if Max knew Sami, his mate was about to put himself in a whole heap of danger.

Oscar Juwani moved. He stepped slowly, wordlessly, around the pit. He stopped immediately behind Sami. 'Get up,' he said.

Sami glanced across the pit at Max. Very faintly – barely a twitch – he winked. Then he stood.

Oscar Juwani grabbed Sami's arm and gave an order to

Katva. With obvious disappointment, Katva pulled Roland away from the pit and let go of him. Oscar Juwani leaned towards Sami and spoke. Max could only just hear him.

'You,' he said, 'are a very stupid boy.'

'Maybe,' Sami said. He turned his head so they were face to face. 'Maybe not. You can decide against this, Oscar Juwani. You can decide to do the right thing, for once in your life.'

'And what is that?'

'It's simple. Free the men in the cage. You have my word that they will not kill you. Free the Blueshirts and the Redshirts. Tell the Blackshirts to turn in their weapons. After that, you must all do exactly as my friends and I tell you. If you do that, you might live to see the dawn.'

Oscar Juwani stared at him. 'You think you can kill me, boy?'

'No,' Sami said. 'My friends and I don't kill people. We save them. We can save you too, if you let us.'

Oscar Juwani burst out laughing. He slapped his thighs and shouted at his thugs, obviously translating what Sami had just said. The Blackshirts, who still had their backs to the jungle, started to laugh too, and so did Katva, although he seemed less sure of himself than the others. The Redshirts and Blueshirts remained silent. Then, as quickly as he had started to laugh, Oscar Juwani shouted, 'The rest of you – move to the end of the pit! I will show you what happens when people speak to Oscar Juwani like that.'

Lukas, Lili and Abby looked uncertain. 'Do it,' Max called. They glanced over at him, then scrambled to their feet and moved to where Katva had been holding Roland. The Blackshirts continued to laugh. Oscar Juwani forced Sami closer to the edge of the pit.

Then Max saw another movement in the jungle, and he fully understood what Sami was up to.

A shape had emerged from the forest, behind the armed Blackshirts, who had their backs to it. It was almost human, but not quite. It was bigger, for a start, and bent double. Max thought he could just make out a streak of silver at the top of its back. The creature stood on its hind legs and roared. Was it the same silverback gorilla they had encountered two days ago on their way through the jungle? Max wondered. Could it be?

Only now he had backup.

Two more gorillas had emerged from the foliage, smaller than the silverback but still enormous and fearsome. They flanked the silverback like two burly lieutenants, rearing up and roaring in the same way.

The effect on the Blackshirts was immediate. They spun round in alarm, then looked back towards the fire, as if checking for an escape route. Their faces were terrified. Oscar Juwani let go of Sami and staggered away from the pit towards his Blackshirts. But that moved him closer to the creatures, who were thundering towards them. There was a sudden, chaotic outburst of panicked shouts.

'Don't look at them!' Sami shouted above the noise. 'Lower your heads! Look at the ground! Don't look at them! Don't run!'

His instructions were for the cadets. Max immediately did as was told. He hung his head and hunched down to make himself look smaller. He glanced ahead. The Blackshirts were still panicking, Oscar Juwani among them. He screamed something, pointing angrily at his Blackshirts and making a 'shoot them' gesture. Max could see Babaka fumbling for his weapon . . .

But it was too late. The three gorillas were among them. Babaka and the others had dropped their weapons and were running away. Oscar Juwani was in the middle of the scrum, screaming. Babaka collided with him, and Oscar Juwani stumbled, staggering towards the pit. Sami was motionless, his head bowed, a picture of calm, close to him. The silverback roared again. It was a terrible sound, louder and more aggressive than before. Max felt it in the pit of his stomach. It seemed to have a similar effect on Babaka, who was closest to the gorilla. He staggered backwards, losing his grip on his weapon, and collided with Oscar Juwani, teetering on the edge of the pit, for a second time.

And it was that second collision with his right-hand man that forced Oscar Juwani over the edge.

The Blackshirts were by the fire. Even Babaka scrambled away from the pit as his leader reeled, windmilling his arms to save himself, but unsuccessfully.

He tumbled into the pit.

There was a split second of absolute silence. Even the gorillas were momentarily still. Then the screaming started.

It hardly sounded human. Oscar Juwani shrieked like an animal in pain. The hissing grew angrier. He expected the screaming to stop quickly. But it didn't. For what seemed like hours, Oscar Juwani's screams of pain continued, accompanied by the awful, frenzied hissing.

Then the silverback reared up again. He roared for a third time, and now there was nothing to keep the Blackshirts there. They all, Babaka included, ran for their lives, ignoring the cadets. The Redshirts and Blueshirts panicked too. They crowded towards the steps leading down from the plateau, some crying, some shouting, all of them desperate to escape the horror.

That left only the cadets, and Roland. Max hadn't moved, despite every muscle in his body screaming at him to run. He was frozen, his head bowed, avoiding eye contact with the gorillas. Lukas, Abby, Lili and Roland did the same. And so did Sami. He was next to the silverback, his head down and his shoulders hunched. The two other gorillas stood on either side of the silverback again, the larger gorilla panting heavily. None of them showed any sign of wanting to chase the Blackshirts, or any interest in the contents of the pit, or in the other cadets. The lesser gorillas stared at the silverback, and the silverback stared at Sami, its head inclined.

It reached out one arm and picked something from Sami's hair.

Then it turned. The other two gorillas turned with it. As quickly as they had appeared, they lumbered back towards the jungle.

And then they were gone.

20

Double Tap

The cadets were stunned into inaction. It was only when Lili stood up that Max felt able to move.

'Did you activate the PLB?' she asked.

'Yes,' Max said. 'If it worked, the Watchers should be on their way.'

'It could take an hour for them to get here,' Abby said. 'Those Blackshirts aren't going to stay scared for long. They're armed. As soon as they regroup, they'll be after us. We can't rely on Sami's hairy friend to rescue us again.'

Max checked the plateau. The fire was subsiding, but there was enough light to see the area was deserted. All the others had escaped into the clearing, from where he could hear shouts.

'Oscar Juwani had weapons in his hut,' Lukas said. 'We can get them.'

'Right,' Abby said. 'We have the high ground. If we have weapons, we can defend the plateau against the Blackshirts till the Watchers arrive.'

The other cadets nodded. All except Max. 'No,' he said.

'Come on, Max,' Abby said. 'I know you don't like using weapons if you don't have to –'

'We need the weapons,' Max interrupted her. 'But we can't let the Blackshirts stay in the clearing. That's where the helicopters will land. If the Blackshirts fire at them, the choppers could crash. We need to draw them away from the landing zone.'

'How?' Sami said.

Max pointed at the area of jungle where the silverback had disappeared. 'There,' he said. 'We enter the jungle with our weapons. We release some rounds. The Blackshirts will think they're under attack. They'll come for us. Then the choppers can land safely.'

Roland had stood up. He was staring at the cadets, blinking. 'Who *are* you?' he said.

'We're just here to help,' Max said. 'Come on, everyone.'

Quickly, he led them across the clearing into Oscar Juwani's hut. It was lit by candles, with rugs and cushions scattered here and there. Max ignored all that and walked straight up to the weapons racks on the wall. He helped himself to an AK-47 assault rifle and five full clips of ammo. The others did the same, all except Roland, who stood in the middle of the hut staring at them. 'Who *are* you?' he repeated.

'We're nobody,' Max said. 'After tonight, you'll never see us again. But listen, Roland, you've got a job to do.' He took a handgun from the wall, checked that it was fully loaded, then made it safe. He handed it to Roland. 'If everything goes according to plan, the Blackshirts will come after us. That'll leave the Redshirts and the Blueshirts in the clearing. They'll be frightened and panicking. You need to keep them busy. There are helicopters coming. They'll need a clear area to land. Get everybody to help.'

'What if they won't do as I say?' Roland asked. 'Some of the Redshirts . . .'

Max pointed at the handgun he'd given Roland.

'Oh,' Roland said. 'I see.'

'You can't *use* it,' Max told him. 'You understand that, right?'

'Of course,' Roland said.

Lukas strode up to him. 'You don't use it on *anyone*,' he said. 'Not even Katva.'

Roland didn't reply.

Lukas's lips thinned. 'Trust me, Roland. The people in the choppers, they *really* don't like seeing young people getting shot. If you're the one who does it . . .' He left the rest to Roland's imagination.

'Come on,' Lili hissed. The sound of shouting in the clearing was getting louder. 'The Blackshirts are coming back. We need to get into the jungle.'

Max put one hand on Roland's shoulder. 'You can do it,' he said. 'Wait till the Blackshirts come after us. Then get down there.'

Roland clenched his jaw and nodded. The cadets hurried

out of the hut. They ran across the plateau, past the fire, past the snake pit. Max could hear Babaka. He was coming up the steps, shouting. The cadets upped their pace and hit the treeline, plunging into the thick darkness of the jungle.

Back at Valley House, they had trained with night-vision goggles. Max would have given almost anything for that kind of capability now. In the trees, it was almost pitch black. Not even the light from the fire penetrated the jungle. The cadets huddled together, waiting for their vision to adjust to the darkness. It took thirty seconds for shapes to form. Jagged branches. Broad leaves. Max's vision had no depth of field, so he couldn't tell what was close and what distant. Moving through this environment would be treacherous.

They had to do it though. The Blackshirts would soon work out where they had gone. Whether they would follow was anybody's guess. Max reckoned they wouldn't – yet. They would just assume that the cadets were lost in the jungle. That wasn't the outcome they needed. If they were to draw the Blackshirts out of the clearing, the cadets needed to present a threat.

Just not here.

'Listen up,' Max whispered. 'Where the log pile is, down in the clearing, that's twelve o'clock as you face it. We head downhill through the jungle to that position. Lukas and I will stay there. Abby, Lili, Sami, move round to nine o'clock. When you're in position, release some rounds, then head back immediately to twelve o'clock. The Blackshirts will think they're being attacked from the nine o'clock direction. We'll give it five minutes, then we'll release rounds from twelve o'clock to disorientate them. Then we'll skirt back round to three o'clock. We don't show ourselves till the Watchers arrive. Everyone agreed?'

Nobody had the chance to reply. A spray of automatic fire burst from the clearing into the jungle. The cadets hit the ground as one.

'Is everyone okay?' Max hissed, adjusting his rifle so it was slung across his back. There were four replies of 'Yes', followed by another burst of fire.

'Crawl,' Max whispered. '*Now!*'

Max didn't know what was more terrifying: the thought that the Blackshirts would fire at them again, or the unknown jungle. He winced every time he placed his palm down on the ground. Try though he might, he couldn't get Oscar Juwani's screams out of his head, or the gruesome sound of him being attacked by his own snakes. He knew those snakes hadn't travelled far, just as he knew that the silverback was surely close by, as well as a hundred other grisly threats. He told himself that the jungle creatures were better adapted to their environment, and would get out of their way. It didn't help much.

Then there was the vegetation. Vines and brambles

seemed to jump out of nowhere, scratching his face, blocking his way. Max sometimes had a dream: no matter how fast he tried to run, he couldn't move. This felt like that, as if the jungle was conspiring to hold him back.

At least there was no more gunfire. The cadets advanced slowly. After a few minutes they got to their feet again. This afforded them a little more speed. The terrain moved downhill, then they spent ten minutes forcing their way through flat ground. He estimated that they were closing in on the twelve o'clock position.

'Wait here, everyone,' Lili whispered. She moved in the direction of the clearing, disappearing for maybe twenty seconds before reappearing again. 'We're in position,' she reported. 'The Blackshirts have rounded everyone up in the centre. I can't see Roland, so I guess he must still be hiding. Max, Lukas, you stay here. The rest of us will move to nine o'clock.'

Without another word, Lili, Abby and Sami moved on, leaving Max and Lukas alone in the darkness.

They didn't speak at first. This was the first time they'd been alone together since Lukas had pretended to shoot the girls. Max had said some pretty terrible things to his friend since then. He knew he had to apologise.

'Mate . . .' he started to say.

'Forget it,' Lukas said. 'If I was you, I'd have said and thought the same. I almost *was* thinking the same. I wasn't sure I hadn't killed them.'

'Even so,' Max said, 'I should have known you'd never do that. It's just . . .'

'What?'

'You seemed like you were in a weird place at the beginning of the operation. You weren't yourself. I thought maybe everything had got on top of you.'

'Maybe it had,' Lukas replied.

Max didn't push it. He figured his friend would open up if he wanted to.

Lukas continued. 'It's just . . . when Hector told us all about Oscar Juwani and Joseph Kony, and their child soldiers and child slaves, it kind of . . .'

'Kind of what?'

'It kind of sounded like me, growing up. My whole life, my whole *family's* life, was gangs. I saw kids with guns every day of the week. Oscar Juwani's just a gang leader. Those Blackshirts, they're just like my old friends. Different part of the world, different language, but not different people. You get me?'

'I think so,' Max said.

'That guy Babaka? He's not so different to me.'

'You're wrong, you know,' Max said. 'You couldn't be less like Babaka if you tried. The gang member who killed your mum and dad? He would be dead if you hadn't done the right thing and turned him in to the police. Babaka *likes* killing people, Lukas. You go out of your way to avoid it, despite everything you've been

181

through. Babaka continues the cycle. You break it.'

'You're wrong,' Lukas said. 'If Babaka was here in front of me, after what he made me do to Lili and Abby . . .' Lukas was silent for a full thirty seconds. When he spoke, his voice wavered a little. 'I think I'd want to kill him.'

'Remember what Sami said to Oscar Juwani, Lukas. We're Special Forces Cadets. We don't kill people. We save them.'

'When the Watchers come, they'll have an SAS team with them. They won't hold back. You know what that means?'

'For the Blackshirts, yes,' Max said.

'So what does it matter who kills them – the SAS or us?'

'It matters,' Max said firmly. 'Trust me, Lukas, it matters. We can still help people.'

'Like who?'

'The Redshirts and the Blueshirts. I don't know about you, but I'm not leaving here until we know they're going to be taken back out of the jungle to safety. They live, Lukas. If you and I have anything to do with it, they live.'

Max listened hard, straining for the sound of approaching choppers, but all he heard was the confused shouting of the Blackshirts – then a burst of fire from the right-hand side of the clearing. A brief silence, then two more bursts. There were ferocious shouts in the clearing, and Max heard Babaka roaring instructions at the others. 'I'm going to check what's happening,' he whispered to Lukas.

He forced his way through the jungle to the edge of the open space. The Blackshirts stood in a line, facing the nine o'clock position, their weapons engaged. The remaining Redshirts and Blueshirts huddled near the cage where Max and Sami had been locked up. There was no sign of Roland. Babaka barked an order. The Blackshirts all fired a single shot into the trees.

'Move,' Max hissed to himself, willing Lili, Abby and Sami to get out of the firing line. The Blackshirts advanced and entered the jungle, moving out of sight. Max maintained his position for a little longer. He saw Roland sprinting down the steps from the plateau towards the Redshirts and Blueshirts.

That was enough. He made his way back to Lukas. 'The Blackshirts have left the clearing,' he said.

'They fired their weapons?'

Max nodded. 'But the others will have been on the move by then.'

They waited in silence. The occasional shout of a Blackshirt deep in the jungle reached them, but nothing else. Max didn't voice the nagging worry in his mind: the watch had been in Babaka's possession for more than a day. Was it still operational? What if the Blackshirt had damaged it? What if the Watchers weren't on their way after all? The cadets couldn't avoid their enemy for ever . . .

Movement, nearby. Max and Lukas engaged their

weapons and peered blindly through the darkness. Max's finger was sweaty on the trigger guard. His lips were dry. He knew people were close, but he didn't know how many or who they were . . .

'It's us.' It was Sami.

Max lowered his weapon. 'Here,' he whispered.

Seconds later, the others were with them.

The cadets stood in a circle, facing outwards, shoulders touching. They raised their weapons at a forty-five degree angle. '*Now!*' Lili said.

They fired. The short, sharp bursts were almost deafening, and the recoil from the automatic rifles jolted sharply against Max's shoulder. He made his weapon safe and lowered it. 'Move back,' he whispered. 'Further into the jungle. They'll be heading this way.'

'I just hope that Roland is clearing a landing zone,' Abby muttered. 'I'd hate to be doing all this for nothing.'

They ploughed further into the jungle, away from the clearing. The shouts of the Blackshirts grew closer. They sounded stressed and confused. They obviously thought they were under attack, but they didn't know where from. It was a volatile situation. The Blackshirts would be scared. And trigger-happy.

'Get down!' Lili hissed. 'They're close.'

The cadets hit the forest floor. Max found himself at the base of a tree trunk, his weapon pointing randomly into the darkness. He could hear his heart thumping. He could also hear someone moving through the foliage. He tried to estimate how close they were. Ten metres? A little less maybe? It was impossible to be accurate in the darkness. He held his breath, trying to keep as still and silent as possible.

Then he heard it.

It was muffled and distant, but there was no doubt that it was the sound of a helicopter – maybe more than one – approaching from behind them. It quickly grew much louder. The Blackshirts started shouting at each other again. The proximity of their voices made Max realise they were closer than he had thought: several of them right nearby. He felt his muscles tensing up, his finger tensing on the trigger.

Then the choppers were almost on top of them. And with the choppers came light. Powerful searchlights, moving at speed, the fierce beams penetrating the canopy. Max winced. A ray of light swung across him, hurting his eyes. But more than that, it lit him up. He heard the Blackshirts shouting again. Another pass of the light illuminated, for a split second, a face. It was Babaka: he had seen Max and he was pointing his weapon right at him.

Darkness. Then gunfire. The sound of Babaka's weapon was ear-splitting. Max expected to feel the bullets penetrating his body. Instead he felt them drum into the tree trunk just above his head. He rolled quickly to the right as a searchlight passed their way again. This time it just missed Max, but he saw Babaka down on one knee, his face wild, his gun swinging from side to side. Standing behind him, his weapon pointing at the back of Babaka's head, was Lukas.

'*Lukas, no!*' Max bellowed. They were all in darkness again. A second burst of fire flew in Max's direction. He could feel the air displacement as the bullets whizzed past his head. And when the searchlight reappeared, lighting up the ground in front of him, Max could no longer see either Babaka or Lukas.

The choppers – Max thought there were three – had passed over. It sounded like they were touching down in the clearing. The jungle was in darkness again, but there was movement all around. Max stayed very still, crouching in the darkness, desperately hoping that none of the Blackshirts would stumble across him. The foliage around him rustled. Branches creaked and snapped underfoot. Then, suddenly, there was the hushed thud of a weapon being discharged twice in quick succession.

Max knew what that meant. The rescue team had arrived.

He lowered his weapon and laid it on the ground. From somewhere behind him, there was another suppressed double tap. Max raised his hands, palms upwards – and not before time. A figure loomed above him. He could just distinguish the outline of a person in full military gear: camo trousers and jacket, bulging ops waistcoat and a

Kevlar helmet with night-vision goggles and boom mic. And a weapon, of course: an assault rifle with a short stock pressed into the soldier's shoulder.

'My name is Max Johnson,' Max whispered. 'I'm a British citizen.'

To his right, there was another double tap. The soldier raised his assault rifle and quickly fired another two rounds. Max heard the unmistakable sound of a body slumping to the ground. Then the soldier held out one hand. Max grabbed it. The soldier pulled him to his feet, then spoke. 'Nice work, Max. Hope these guys in the black shirts weren't friends of yours.'

It was a female voice.

'*Angel?*' He felt suddenly drenched with relief.

Angel didn't reply. She raised her weapon again and fired two more shots. Another body hit the ground. 'Some kid in the clearing said it's the ones in black shirts who are armed. How many are there?' she demanded.

'Fifteen in total.'

Angel spoke into the boom mic. 'This is Alpha three. We have fifteen targets in black shirts. Confirming five kills.' She cocked her head and listened. Somewhere, a little further off, Max heard more gunfire.

'We have nine targets down,' she said to Max. 'Sami, Lili and Abby are safe. There's no sign of Lukas yet.'

Max felt sick. 'Last time I saw him, he was with Babaka – Oscar Juwani's right-hand guy.'

'And Oscar Juwani?'

'Dead,' Max said.

'How?'

'You don't want to know.'

'Get back to the clearing. No heroics, Max. I'm going after this Babaka guy.'

'Angel, find him quickly. If you don't, I think Lukas might try to kill him . . . .'

'Get to the clearing,' Angel said, and she melted back into the darkness.

Max stumbled through the jungle, following the sound of rotor blades and the shards of light penetrating the jungle from the clearing. He ignored the thorns cutting his face and the scurrying creatures fleeing his path. He just wanted to be out of the jungle, away from all the horrors it contained.

He burst out into the clearing by the log pile. Sami, Lili and Abby were there, crouched down behind the logs. Three Chinooks had touched down. Their double rotors were still spinning, kicking dust up into the air which sparked against the blades, causing a strange circular glow. The tailgates were open. In the air, circling the clearing, was an Apache attack helicopter, its guns and missiles visible. Soldiers, heavily armed, swarmed through the clearing, shouting instructions and securing the area. All the Redshirts and Blueshirts were on the ground, face-down. Max tried to pick out Roland, but couldn't see him amid the confusion. Then he looked over towards the suspended cage, where the SAS hostages were being held. There was much activity and torchlight here. The huts blocked Max's view of the ground, but he could see the cage being lowered.

'They're not going to be in a good way,' said a voice behind Max. 'But as far as we can tell, they're alive, just. Thanks to you lot.'

Max turned. Hector stood there. He was dressed as Angel had been, in military camo and night-vision goggles, though these were perched on the top of his helmet.

'Lukas –' Max started to say.

'Angel and Woody will find him,' Hector said firmly.

Max pointed into the clearing. 'The Redshirts and Blueshirts,' he said, 'you mustn't shoot any of them.'

'They'll all be fine. We're airlifting them to safety. They'll get the help and support they need. We were beginning to worry about you guys. How come you didn't activate the PLB earlier?'

'Long story . . .' Max started to say, then fell silent. Two figures had just emerged from the treeline. Babaka first, his hands on his head. And behind him, his assault rifle pointing at the back of Babaka's skull, was Lukas. Angel and Woody burst into the clearing, clearly searching for something. When they saw Lukas and Babaka, they stopped.

Babaka was sweating, but there was a fierce madness

to him, along with his usual arrogance, as if he didn't care whether he lived or died. Lukas seemed calm and determined. His finger lay lightly on the trigger of his rifle. He was a few millimetres away from taking a life – for real, this time.

Max stood up and walked towards Lukas. They stared at each other.

'You're not that person, Lukas,' Max said. 'We all know that. You're the only one who doubts it.'

Lukas lowered his head. Max thought he was going to shoot. But then he kicked Babaka in the back of the knee. The Blackshirt fell to his knees and Lukas lowered his weapon. 'Nobody is to shoot him,' he announced. 'I want him to rot in jail.' He turned away from his prisoner as Hector ran up and bound Babaka's hands behind his back.

Max strode up to his friend, wanting to shake his hand. Then Lili cried out 'Roland!' and Abby swore. At the top of the steps leading to the plateau was Katva the Redshirt, on his knees. Roland had a gun to his head.

'Roland,' Max whispered, 'don't do it.' He turned to the others. 'Come with me!' he shouted.

The cadets sprinted across the clearing towards the steps. Max took them two at a time, hurtling up to Roland and Katva, his friends on his heel.

'Stand back!' Roland shouted when Max was up on the plateau. 'I don't want to hurt you too.' His gun hand shook and his face was damp with sweat. The barrel of his handgun was almost touching the back of Katva's head. Katva was trembling too.

'Mate,' Max said, 'seriously, you don't need to –'

But before he could finish, Lukas had shoulder-barged him out of the way. 'Go ahead,' he said. 'Shoot him.'

Roland's hand shook a bit more.

'Seriously,' Lukas said. 'nobody's going to stop you. But before you pull that trigger, have a think about what happens next. Maybe Katva has a brother of his own. Or a sister. Maybe his mum and dad are still alive. What will they do if they find out how he died? Shrug their shoulders and think, *Whatever*?'

Roland swallowed hard. He remained silent.

'Or will they want revenge, just like you did? How many people will they want to kill to get it? Just you, or you and your family? Or you and your friends? Or just some random, innocents who have nothing to do with this?'

'You expect me to forgive him?' Roland asked, his voice little more than a whisper. 'What about justice?'

Lukas stepped a little closer. 'Justice and retribution aren't the same thing, Roland. Trust me. I've seen what happens when people get them mixed up.' He glanced back at Max, then at Roland again. 'You can break the cycle,' he said. 'You can do your bit to stop the violence. All you have to do is step back and lower your gun.'

'He's right, Roland,' Abby called over the sound of the choppers. 'Shooting him achieves nothing.'

There was a pause. Then Roland fired his weapon. Three rounds, in quick succession, so close and loud that Max almost felt as if he had been shot.

But he hadn't been. And nor had Katva. Roland had emptied the weapon into the ground. He kicked Katva in the small of the back. Katva collapsed. Roland walked up to Lukas and handed him the weapon. 'I never want to see another gun in my life,' he said.

Epilogue

The next few hours were a blur of activity. Babaka, Katva and two other Blackshirts were held under armed guard. The remainder were brought out of the jungle and placed in body bags. Two of the Chinooks airlifted the prisoners, the body bags and half the Blueshirts and Redshirts out of the jungle before returning to continue the evacuation. A temporary medical tent was set up near the plateau. Max saw the SAS prisoners being stretchered into it for immediate attention, and with a twist of anxiety in his stomach he realised he had forgotten about the kid with the septic hands. He searched the clearing with a rising sense of panic until he found the little boy sitting by the half-burned log pile, clutching his knees and shivering. The boy didn't seem to know where he was. Max wasn't even sure he was aware of Max's presence. He bent down, scooped him up in his arms – the boy's body was burning up – and carried him across the clearing to the medical tent.

Inside the tent, three medics were tending to the SAS men under the glare of some portable lights. The captured soldiers were gaunt, their faces covered with sores, their eyes bloodshot. They smelled foul. But they were alive. Just.

One of the medics turned to Max. Max thought he was about to chide him, but then he saw the state of the boy in Max's arms. 'What's wrong with him?' he asked.

'Infection,' Max said, 'I think. From his hands. He's been getting worse.'

The medic nodded. 'Leave him with us. We'll clean him up, get some antibiotics into him.' He took the boy from Max. 'You have to leave. Medical personnel only.'

Max nodded. He gave the kid one final look, and left the tent.

Outside, more children were being loaded into the Chinooks. Sami, Lukas, Abby and Lili were helping Woody, Angel and several other soldiers lead them into the choppers. Hector was waiting outside the medical tent. His face was grubby, his beard wet with sweat and humidity. 'Who's the kid you just took in there?' he said.

'I . . . I don't know his name,' Max said. 'He was in a bad way.'

'They'll do their best for him.'

'What if their best isn't enough?'

Hector gave him a steady stare. Max bowed his head.

'You saved some lives today, Max. That's getting to be a habit for you and your team. Your dad would be proud.'

'We lost some lives too.'

Hector nodded. 'Sometimes,' he said, 'you can't do

one without doing the other. At the end of the day, that's what soldiering's all about.'

'We nearly lost our own lives.'

'Sometimes, *that's* what soldiering is all about too.' He put a hand on Max's shoulder. 'Look on the bright side,' he said. 'You haven't killed anybody yet. Although young Lukas came close, from what I hear. He and I will need a discussion about that little strategy of his.'

There was something ominous about the word 'yet', and Max found he didn't want to continue the conversation. Fortunately there was a distraction: the sound of another helicopter arriving. It was a Sea King, smaller than the Chinooks. The pilot deftly set it down in the clearing.

'That's our lift,' Hector said. 'The SAS squadron will take it from here.'

'Hector, I'd . . .'

'What?'

'I'd like to do something for Roland. Get him away from all this. Can't we, I don't know, take him with us?'

Hector gave him a long look. 'You think you haven't done something for him already?'

'But –'

'Think how many lives you've changed for the better today,' Hector said. 'You'll have to learn to let that be enough.' He gave Max a piercing look. 'Anyway, what makes you think Roland would want to leave his home. Valley House would be as strange to him as this place is to you.'

'I guess, but . . .'

'No buts, Max. We're a special forces unit, not an orphanage. Get used to it.'

Hector walked towards the Sea King and Max followed, slightly reluctantly. The other cadets approached from different directions. Max watched them carefully. Lukas seldom smiled, and now was no exception, but Max could tell from his body language that the tension he had been carrying for the last two days had left him. Abby's brow was furrowed, her expression sharp – a reminder that behind the wisecracks she was as serious and professional as the rest of them. Lili walked rather than ran, apparently as calm as she always was, no matter what was going on around her. And Sami: brave, trusting Sami. He was small, but he walked tall across the clearing, with the confidence of a young man who knew he had made good choices. Risky choices, Max thought. But good. And effective.

Halfway to the Sea King, Max stopped. Roland stood by one of the Chinooks, watching the cadets as they approached the Sea King. Their eyes met. Roland inclined his head and, across the clearing, he mouthed, 'Thank you.'

Max nodded and raised one hand in farewell. Roland turned and continued to help the younger kids. Max jogged towards the Sea King. The other cadets were already climbing inside with Hector, Woody and Angel.

A profound tiredness crashed over him as the chopper powered up. Dawn was breaking, and as they rose above the treetops he could see the vast Congo rainforest stretching to the horizon, gently bathed in the glowing light of the rising sun.

'Beautiful, isn't it?' Abby said.

'Yeah,' Max replied. 'Beautiful.' But he didn't enjoy the sight for long. Within seconds, he had fallen asleep.

Chris Ryan

Chris Ryan was born in Newcastle.

In 1984 he joined 22 SAS. After completing the year-long Alpine Guides Course, he was the troop guide for B Squadron Mountain Troop. He completed three tours with the anti-terrorist team, serving as an assaulter, sniper and finally Sniper Team Commander.

Chris was part of the SAS eight-man patrol chosen for the famous Bravo Two Zero mission during the 1991 Gulf War. He was the only member of the unit to escape from Iraq, where three of his colleagues were killed and four captured. This was the longest escape and evasion in the history of the SAS, and for this he was awarded the Military Medal. Chris wrote about his experiences in his book *The One That Got Away*, which was adapted for screen and became an immediate bestseller.

Since then he has written four other books of non-fiction, over twenty bestselling novels and three series of children's books. Chris's novels have gone on to inspire the Sky One series *Strike Back*.

In addition to his books, Chris has presented a number of very successful TV programmes including *Hunting Chris Ryan*, *How Not to Die* and *Chris Ryan's Elite Police*.

Want to read
NEW BOOKS
before anyone else?

Like getting
FREE BOOKS?

Enjoy sharing your
OPINIONS?

Discover

READERS FIRST

Read. Love. Share.

Get your first free book just by signing up at
readersfirst.co.uk

For Terms and Conditions see readersfirst.co.uk/pages/terms-of-service

HOT KEY BOOKS

Thank you for choosing a Hot Key book.

If you want to know more about our authors and what we publish, you can find us online.

You can start at our website

www.hotkeybooks.com

And you can also find us on:

We hope to see you soon!